Mr. Mansfield was brushing Stormy when Melissa burst in. The big gray nickered and moved his ears, but her dad didn't even turn around.

"Dad, I want to help find Scott," Melissa said.

Chuck Mansfield was a tall man with thick, sandy hair and a matching mustache. He curried his horse with quick strong strokes. "I haven't time to talk now, Missy," he said.

"I've got a personal stake in this Dad. Scott is my responsibility."

"Why didn't you think of that last night?" Her dad's usually smiling eyes were ice blue, the color of the January day.

BABY-SITTER
ON
HORSEBACK

Fern G. Brown

FAWCETT JUNIPER • NEW YORK

RLI: $\dfrac{\text{VL 6 \& up}}{\text{IL 6 \& up}}$

A Fawcett Juniper Book
Published by Ballantine Books
Copyright © 1988 by Fern Brown

Library of Congress Catalog Card Number: 88-91166

ISBN 0-449-70283-9

Manufactured in the United States of America

First Edition: November 1988

DEDICATION

This book is dedicated to the Mansfield Family, and especially to Melissa.

ACKNOWLEDGMENTS

The author and editor wish to thank the following for their valuable assistance in the preparation of this book.

County Sheriff's Office, Lake County, Illinois; Lake County Mounted Posse, Lake County, Illinois; Andrew Zambory, Former Chief of Police, Wickliffe, Ohio; Leonard J. Brown; and Marion M. Markham.

CHAPTER 1

Friday, 5:45 P.M.

The familiar snow-covered trail was scary in the dark. Melissa Mansfield shivered as gusts of icy wind howled through bare branches. The path was a short cut to the Robinsons' where she was going to baby-sit for Scott. She didn't want to be late again but these days she always seemed to goof up—like when she left her hair dryer plugged in and her mother tripped over the cord and broke her ankle.

Although Melissa only had to walk a few blocks, the wind and deep snow that night made it seem like miles. At last she smelled the odor of horses, and saw the outline of the Robinsons' barn between the trees.

Then she heard it—a cracking, snapping sound in the woods. A shadow from behind fell across the path! Melissa's heart pounded like horses' hooves at a full gallop.

She spun around and the blinding beam of a flashlight hit her face. She let out a frightened gasp. "Who's there?"

"Melissa?"

1

The voice came from right in front of her and she almost jumped out of her skin.

It was Scott Robinson.

"Don't shine that light in my eyes," she said.

Scott clicked off his light. He was a small boy with big front teeth and a scrawny neck, who looked younger than his ten years.

"You scared me to death," Melissa told him. "I'm still shaking."

"Sorry. I was in the barn," said Scott, "and I heard a noise out here."

"What were you doing in the barn after dark?"

"Nosey is sick." Nosey was Scott's spotted mare.

"What's wrong?"

He shrugged. "She won't eat." Scott's voice matched his looks, thin and frail.

As they walked toward the house, Melissa drew her collar tight around her neck. The wind blew out of the north, and they went forward together, heads lowered, clutching their jackets against the cold.

"Did you call the vet?" Melissa asked.

"Montana did. But Doc can't come until tomorrow." Montana was the barn man who had been part of Scott's life since he was a baby.

"Nosey is strong. She'll be okay," said Melissa.

Scott and Melissa loved horses, and they were both good riders. When a blast of wind whipped the flag around the pole Melissa looked up. For a fleeting second she thought she saw a shape near the barn. It was probably just blowing snow. Still, she put her arm around Scott. She always worried about him. His mother had died when he was three. Mr. Robinson tried to hire good housekeepers, but even a great housekeeper couldn't replace a mother.

When they reached the house, the porch light flooded the

yard. Pointed icicles under the eaves glistened like crystal daggers.

"Oh, there you are, Melissa." A plump, middle-aged woman stood in the doorway. It was Mrs. Seliber, the Robinsons' current housekeeper. Whenever Mrs. Seliber visited her sister overnight, Melissa stayed with Scott until his father came home.

"Come in you two," Mrs. Seliber's voice boomed. "Scott, you'll catch your death of cold. No horse in the world is worth pneumonia."

Melissa and Scott exchanged glances. Mrs. Seliber didn't understand how wonderful it was to canter along a wooded trail on the back of your own horse. She didn't know the great feeling of having an animal to love and care for, one that trusted you and reciprocated your love—sometimes more than humans did.

As Melissa took off her knit hat, Mrs. Seliber said, "You've cut your hair. I like it short."

"Thanks." Melissa smiled and hung her jacket on the kitchen doorknob.

She'd cut her hair this week because she worried a lot about what people thought of her. She didn't want to look like every other blue-eyed blonde in the high school junior class with shoulder-length hair and bangs. She'd hoped this style made her look older than sixteen—more dependable.

"Your frozen dinners are in the oven," Mrs. Seliber told them. "And Scott, your father called. He's working late again tonight—some kind of meeting in the city. I Left the number near the phone." She buttoned her fake fur coat. "But he'll try to get home before you go to bed."

Melissa saw the sadness in Scott's eyes deepen. "All my father ever does is work," he said softly.

"If your father didn't work hard, you couldn't have a horse and live in a place like this, my boy." Mrs. Seliber gestured with her arms wide. Her voice bounded off the walls like a boomerang.

Melissa understood what Mrs. Seliber meant. The Robinsons' kitchen was twice the size of the Mansfields' and filled with all the latest gadgets.

After the housekeeper left, they went into the family room. It was two stories high with narrow floor-to-ceiling windows looking out over the snow-covered woods. Scott flopped into a brown leather chair.

Melissa tried to make him forget about Nosey. "Want to hear a story about the sheriff's posse?" she asked.

Scott nodded.

In Woodvale, Illinois, where they lived, the county sheriff had a civilian horse posse made up of neighbors who rode. The posse was called out to help the sheriff's men search the woods for missing persons or animals. Melissa's father and their neighbor Roscoe Cannon were the leaders, and her best friend, Kory McCormack, was a member.

Melissa perched on a footstool. "Well," she began, "this is a true story. Once, there was this horse that jumped the fence and got lost in the woods. My father . . ."

Telling the story made Melissa think about how much she wanted to ride with them. More than anything in the whole world she wanted to be a posse member, too. Recently Daniel Simcoe, a wimp in her class, had joined. She was a better rider than Daniel, but her father had said that before *she* could join she had to prove that she was reliable. Dad hadn't forgotten last fall when she'd left the stall door unlocked and Stormy, his Arabian, had run out. The horse had trampled the front lawn and chewed several evergreens before he was corralled. She was still paying every week for new trees. There were other things she'd done that her parents weren't happy about, too, like losing her new down-filled jacket and leaving the TV on all day when no one was home. She was trying to organize her life and be a reliable person but . . .

Melissa realized that she had stopped talking to Scott. No matter. He wasn't listening anyway.

"Hey, Scott!"

He jumped.

"I'm starved. How about dinner near the fire?"

"Sure."

"Then we can watch that mystery on TV," she said.

"Okay," said Scott, without his usual enthusiasm.

Mysteries were their favorite programs. They tried to solve the cases before the TV detective did. Although Melissa was six years older, Scott often figured out the answer first.

Tonight he didn't even try.

"Your mind isn't on TV," she said.

"Yeah, I know."

"Worried about Nosey?"

"Uh huh."

"Once Butterball had colic. I thought my horse would never get well," she said. "But he's in great shape now."

Scott paced up and back. Then he crossed the room and stared gloomily out the window.

Melissa said, "There's nothing to see. It's too dark."

Still he stood there staring.

"Nosey will be all right." When Scott didn't answer Melissa tapped his shoulder. "Better get ready for bed."

"Not yet. I couldn't sleep," he finally replied.

"Hey guy, you can't stare out the window all night."

He turned and looked at Melissa. "I want to go out to the barn."

"Now?"

"Just to see Nosey. Give her a treat or something. Then I'll be able to sleep."

"It's too late," Melissa protested. "And the wind is fierce."

"I'm not afraid," he almost whispered.

She shook her head. "I wouldn't go out there again. And neither should you."

"You can watch from the window, Melissa. Please! I won't be long." His lip began to quiver. Scott really loved his little appaloosa mare.

She looked at his mournful face. Melissa knew she shouldn't let Scott go to the barn this late. Tomorrow would be time enough to visit Nosey. Yet, when Butterball was sick, Melissa never went to bed without checking on him.

"I'll go with you," she said. "Put on your warm jacket. And get a scarf."

Scott hurried into his heavy clothing. Melissa tied the bright red scarf under his collar to keep his neck warm.

As she reached for her jacket, the phone rang.

It was Mrs. Seliber. She'd forgotten to take a roast out of the freezer for the next night's dinner.

Melissa said, "I was just going to the barn with Scott."

Mrs. Seliber kept talking. "It's a rib roast. In the garage freezer. On top. Left side."

Damn, Melissa thought. Why did I answer the phone? "Okay," she said. "I'll take it out when I come back."

"Do it now before you forget," Mrs. Seliber told her.

Scott leaned over and whispered, "I'm too warm with all this stuff on. I'll start for the barn. The light will be a signal that I'm okay."

Melissa put her hand over the mouthpiece and said, "All right. But keep the scarf tied. I'm responsible for you and I don't want you to catch cold."

The door slammed behind Scott.

When Mrs. Seliber finally hung up, Melissa went to the

garage freezer and took out the roast. "That housekeeper!" she muttered. "Sure is bossy."

Melissa put the roast on the sink to defrost. Then she walked to the kitchen window. It was inky black outside. She couldn't see Scott, but the light was on in the barn. He was all right. She started to put on her jacket and hesitated.

Why go out now? Scott would only be gone a minute. Besides, it was as cold as Siberia outside. She would make a cup of hot chocolate to warm him up.

Melissa listened uneasily for Scott's footsteps while she waited for the milk to simmer. It was foolish to worry. Scott knew his way around. He'd be fine. And the barn was only a hundred yards away.

When the chocolate was ready, she looked at her watch. Scott had been gone fifteen minutes. It shouldn't take this long to give Nosey a carrot. Melissa felt a knot in her stomach.

She put on her jacket and flew out the door, tugging at the zipper as she ran. On the way to the barn Melissa shouted, "Scott! What's going on?"

The howling wind was her only answer.

She flung open the door. "Scott! Scott Robinson!"

A chorus of nickers greeted her. Four horses leaned over their stall doors. The light was still on, but Scott wasn't there.

"All right, Scott," Melissa called, "I know you're hiding. You can come out now."

Silence.

Melissa walked to Nosey's stall. "Let me in, girl," she said quietly.

Nosey's ears came forward and she whinnied softly. With trembling fingers, Melissa unlatched the stall door, slid it open, and stepped inside. The horse moved close to have her soft nostrils rubbed and her ears stroked.

Melissa reached up to pat the mare, but an object on the stall floor caught her eye.

She gasped.

There, covered with wood shavings, looking like a river of blood, was Scott's bright red scarf!

"Scott!" she called. This time there was a tremor in her voice.

The horses nickered restlessly. Mr. Robinson's bay Thoroughbred gelding, Fever, kicked his stall boards.

At that some moment, a banging noise startled Melissa. She jerked around. "Scott! Is that you?"

The noise repeated. She shivered. But it was only a barn shutter loosened by the wind.

Stay calm, she told herself. Maybe Scott is acting out something he saw on a TV mystery. She picked up the scarf, wound it around her neck, and searched the barn and hayloft. There was nothing.

Grabbing a flashlight from its hook, she went outside.

"Okay, you really scared me," she called into the wind. "Now the game is over. Where are you?" She shone the flashlight into the dark corral. Slowly she moved the beam, lighting every snow-covered corner. Empty.

Quickly Melissa circled the outside of the barn. There were dozens of footprints and hoofprints in the snow. Could there have been a scuffle here? It seemed so. But even with the flashlight it was difficult to see much.

If only stupid Mrs. Seliber hadn't called, Melissa thought. One more minute and she would have been in the barn with Scott. Her hand shook as she tried to keep the light steady. Scott was her responsibility, and she had failed again. She remembered the shape near the barn earlier this evening. Had someone been lurking in the shadows—waiting for Scott?

As cold as it was, Melissa felt as if she'd been struck by a hot branding iron. There might have been nothing—nobody there. But her sixth sense told her otherwise.

She turned and ran. Ran down the path. Ran into the house. Ran to the phone and punched the number the housekeeper had left. The click and buzz of a phone ringing sounded far away. In a few seconds she heard Mr. Robinson's voice. "Hello."

"Mr. Robinson, this is Melissa."

"Melissa? What's wrong?"

"Something awful happened," she blurted. She began to sob and had difficulty speaking. "Scott. It's Scott. He's . . . Mr. Robinson, he's . . ."

Mr. Robinson's voice was curt and businesslike. "Slow down, Melissa. What about Scott?"

"He's gone!"

"He's *what*?"

"Gone. Scott is gone." Breathlessly she explained what had happened. "Scott's scarf was lying in the stall. But he was gone!"

"Melissa, now listen. You're sure he wasn't hiding?"

"I looked. The barn was empty. Should I call the police?"

There was a pause. Then Mr. Robinson said, "Not yet. Scott's run away before."

Melissa said, "I'll go out and look again."

"Stay put until I get there. I'll be right home."

Melissa hung up. Never before had the Robinsons' house seemed so large. And empty.

CHAPTER 2

Friday, 11:00 P.M.

Melissa sat near the family-room fireplace clutching Scott's red scarf. Mr. Robinson bent over her. She jumped, nearly knocking his thick-lensed glasses off his nose.

Mr. Robinson held her shoulder. "Did Scott say anything about running away?" He was a stern man, square-jawed and unsmiling.

Melissa shook her head. He had every right to be angry. She was responsible for Scott, and now he was gone.

Mr. Robinson said, "Scott's been feeling neglected lately. A phase he's going through."

"He wasn't happy that you had to work tonight," she managed.

"Important meeting. I wish I had more time for him, but . . . well, I'm sure he's hiding," said Mr. Robinson, his tone less menacing. "When did you last see him?"

"Bedtime. He went to the barn."

"Why did you let him do that—so late?"

"Nosey is sick."

As Melissa told Mr. Robinson about the evening's events his stern face got darker and angrier. "I trusted you," he said. "I believed you were a responsible person. Why didn't you go to the barn with him?" he demanded.

Melissa felt tears forming again. She felt humiliated—afraid. She never did anything right. Nobody could depend on her. And nobody would ever again.

Mr. Robinson straightened up. "How long was the boy out alone?"

"Fifteen minutes. I looked everywhere. Everywhere! I saw a place where the snow was trampled, but no Scott." Melissa's tears became sobs.

Mr. Robinson cupped his chin and looked thoughtful. She could see the muscles around his mouth tighten.

"Did you search the hayloft?"

"Yes. First thing."

"He might have been hiding in the woods and climbed up to the loft after you went inside. I'm going to check again."

Mr. Robinson took a flashlight and went out.

Melissa stood rooted. Then she grabbed Scott's scarf, yanked on her jacket, and ran after him.

It was sleeting now. She hunched her shoulders inside her jacket and pulled her hat over her ears. The wind nipped at her nose and blew loose snow down her back. Melissa wrapped Scott's scarf around her neck and tried to hurry, but the sleeting snow made walking difficult.

Inside the barn, Melissa heard restless pawing. When the lights went on, the sleepy-eyed horses peered into the aisle, blinking and staring.

Mr. Robinson shined the flashlight into the hayloft.

"Scott!"

Nosey gave a loud nicker at the sound of Mr. Robinson's voice. But there was no answer from the hayloft.

"I've had enough of your nonsense. Do I have to come

up and get you?" Mr. Robinson sounded angry again. "Hold the flashlight, Melissa. Shine it into the loft."

He started up the ladder.

"Hold it steady," he said sharply. "Over there. Left corner. I think I see someone hiding."

After a moment he said, "No. It's just a bale of hay at a crazy angle."

When Scott's father backed down the ladder, Melissa's heart sank. He looked so worried.

They searched the snow-covered corral again. Melissa showed Mr. Robinson where she'd seen the footprints. But now the sleet and snow had covered them.

Finally Mr. Robinson said tersely, "It's late. I'll take you home. Scott will probably be here by the time I get back."

The ride was short and silent. As she left the car Mr. Robinson said, "Scott's tried this before, you know. But he's never stayed out all night. If he doesn't came home by morning, I'll call the sheriff."

Her parents were asleep. Melissa was relieved. Even if Scott did come home it would be hard to face them tomorrow and admit that she'd let him run away again.

Melissa didn't sleep much that night. She trembled beneath the blankets, trying to convince herself that Scott had come home safe and sound. Except that down deep she was afraid that it wasn't true. She wished with all her heart that Scott would be found soon, and if they allowed her to baby-sit again, she'd never, never, ever let him out of her sight.

Too late Melissa realized that she'd forgotten to tell Mr. Robinson about the shape behind the barn. Gloom settled in her belly like spoiled oats.

Toward morning Melissa fell into a restless sleep. She awoke about six o'clock with a sinking sensation. It took only a moment to remember why. She stared up at the ceiling, her mind going over last night's events.

The phone in her parents' room shrilled into her thoughts. Why would anyone call so early? Unless it was bad news . . .

Melissa threw back the covers and ran barefooted into the cold hall. She heard her father's voice behind the closed door.

"I don't believe it," he said. "When?"

"What happened, Chuck?" her mother asked in a muffled half-asleep voice. "What's wrong?"

"Shhh. Tell you in a minute," her father said. "And nobody's seen him since, sheriff?"

The sheriff!

Melissa's knees were shaking. She held on to the wall to steady herself. *SCOTT HAD NOT COME HOME!*

"I'll call Roscoe and the others. We'll saddle up immediately," said her father.

Melissa staggered to her room and into bed. A picture of Scott flashed through her mind. His mournful look—cold without his red scarf—his lips blue and quivering. She buried her face in the pillow.

Someone was knocking.

"Melissa?"

Her mother came in. Connie Mansfield wore a warm velour robe, the color of a ripe peach. The collar was up and the belt was pulled tightly about her waist. She sat on the edge of the bed. Her usually neat brown hair looked as if she hadn't bothered to run a comb through it.

"Sheriff Leonard called out the posse. To look for Scott," she said quietly. Her breath smelled of toothpaste.

Melissa sat up. "He only went to the barn for a few minutes. But he never came back."

"Why did you let him go out alone, Melissa? You should have gone with him," her mother said.

"I know. I know. I'm so sorry." Melissa flung herself into her mother's arms. "Oh, Mom. I'd do anything to change last night. I'm so miserable. If anything happens to Scott, I'll die!"

Mrs. Mansfield stroked Melissa's hair. "They'll find him, hon," she whispered. "They've got to find him."

Melissa rubbed her face against her mother's soft velour robe and for a few moments she had that safe feeling she used to have as a child.

When Mrs. Mansfield had gone, Melissa came back to reality. She wasn't a child anymore. She had to accept responsibility for what had happened. There was only one thing for her to do—if her dad would let her. She dressed hurriedly and walked toward the barn. The sun reflecting on the snow made her squint. She put on her sunglasses.

Mr. Mansfield was brushing Stormy when Melissa burst in. The big gray nickered and moved his ears, but her dad didn't even turn around.

"Dad, I want to help find Scott," Melissa said.

Chuck Mansfield was a tall man with thick, sandy hair and a matching mustache. He curried and brushed his horse with quick, strong strokes. "I haven't time to talk now, Missy," he said.

"I've got a personal stake in this, Dad. Scott is my responsibility."

"Why didn't you think of that last night?" Her dad's usually smiling eyes were ice blue, the color of the January day.

"If only Mrs. Seliber hadn't called—it all happened so fast. You've got to let me go."

Mr. Mansfield hurried into the tack room and returned with blankets and saddle.

Melissa dropped on a hay bale. "Please, Dad. Sheriff Leonard needs all the help he can get. I'm a good rider. I know every inch of the woods. Would it hurt if I rode along?" She tried hard to keep her voice from quivering.

Was her father changing his mind? Melissa held her breath. This was her chance to do something right—like finding Scott.

"Well—the chief investigator for the county police wants to question you at Robinson's house. So I guess you can ride that far."

Mr. Mansfield slid open the barn door and little wisps of hay whirled over the wooden floor. "But I can't wait for you. I've got to organize the riders. Every minute counts."

Melissa jumped up. "I'll have Butterball ready in two minutes. And after I've talked to the investigator—can I ride with you?"

"All right. But hurry."

Melissa had never brushed, saddled, and bridled her little palomino quicker. She fastened his tie-down hurriedly, buttoned her jacket collar and led the horse outside to the snow-covered mounting block. Scraping the snow away with her boot, she mounted.

As soon as she settled into the saddle, she noticed that Butterball kept his head bent in a peculiar way. Leaning over, Melissa discovered that she'd fastened the tie-down that kept him from throwing his head to the throat latch instead of to the noseband. There was no time to dismount and do it over. The posse would leave, and she didn't want them to go without her. Butterball would be okay until she rode to the Robinsons'. It wasn't that far.

Melissa kneed her horse into a walk. The wind was calm, but it was colder than the day before, and there were inches of new snow covering the back trail. She signaled Butterball to trot, but he wasn't his usual frisky self. In this weather, she usually had to hold him down. Maybe it was the deep snow.

"C'mon boy." She urged the little palomino forward. The posse wouldn't wait.

Just as they reached a snow bank her horse bobbed his head and pawed the snow. Butterball was going to lie down! She pulled the reins to keep his head up but he went down on his front knees. When Melissa jumped off, Butterball jerked his head back and broke the rein. Then he scrambled to his feet.

"You dumb horse!" she screamed. "You broke the rein! How can I ride with a lousy broken rein?" Melissa was so angry she wanted to punch Butterball.

Then she felt a lump in her throat. It wasn't Butterball's fault and she knew it. Why hadn't she taken the time to fix the tie-down? Irresponsible, they'd say again.

Melissa blew her nose. No use standing there, her fingers and toes were beginning to feel numb. She took off the bridle, haltered Butterball and led him home on foot.

As she neared the barn she heard a horse nicker behind her.

"Are you all right, Missy?" her father shouted.

She cringed at his voice.

Her dad had left the posse and come all the way back, thinking that she might be in trouble. Now he was wasting precious time waiting for her to answer. What should she say? She pictured his warm, blue eyes icing up again when he heard what had happened.

There was no way out. Melissa took a deep breath. Slowly, very slowly, she turned to face him.

CHAPTER 3

Saturday: 8:00 A.M.

As Mr. Mansfield listened to her story his jaw clenched and his eyes narrowed. Melissa had never seen her father so angry. "You're definitely not riding with the posse," he said. "Take my braided reins and get over to Mike Robinson's house. Pronto!" He plunged his spurs into Stormy's flanks, whirled the horse around and cantered away.

A spatter of snow stung Melissa's face. She dabbed at her cheek with a tissue. How stupid she'd been not to take time to rehook the tie-down. It was because she was so worried about Scott. If they didn't find the boy soon, nothing would ever be right with her life again. This time when she bridled Butterball she hooked the tie-down carefully and then took off.

At the Robinson house, the smell of saddle soap and leather hung on the crisp air as the posse members and their horses gathered in the yard. Melissa saw her dad and his coleader Roscoe Cannon, a robust, bearded man in his late

17

thirties, check the cinches under their horses' bellies. The Brown twins, Stacey and Allison, seniors at school, waved to her.

Kory McCormack and her father were trying to settle Julep, Kory's black Morgan. Julep threw his head and reared, upsetting Mr. and Mrs. Johnsons' mounts. Everyone seemed tense, even the horses.

Finally Julep calmed down and Kory, slender and petite even in her bulky down jacket, came over to talk to Melissa. "It's awful about Scott's disappearance, Missy. I know how terrible you must feel." Kory squinted because of her new contacts. She was always putting her finger on the bridge of her nose as if she were feeling for her glasses. But her dark eyes underneath the bangs were sincerely troubled as she looked up at Melissa. She was a good friend.

"Sorry I didn't call you last night, Kory," Melissa said, "I was too upset."

Kory shrugged. "No big deal. Gotta go. Julep is acting up again."

As Kory walked toward her horse, Mr. Robinson came out in the yard, glasses in hand. He looked as if he hadn't slept. Seeing him reinforced the feeling of guilt Melissa had had ever since Scott's disappearance.

Daniel Simcoe slouched over to talk to her dad, and Melissa felt a stab of resentment. Daniel's arms hung as if they were Scotch taped to his bony frame. Melissa was tall, but Daniel's legs were unending. "Creep!" she muttered, as she tethered Butterball to the hitching post. That miserable beanpole can't ride as well as I can, she thought.

Melissa's father motioned for her to come across the yard.

"Lieutenant Edward Krinn is Chief Investigator for the county, Melissa," her dad said. "He's here to ask you some questions."

Cold sweat ran down her back as the broad-shouldered, graying lieutenant stepped forward. He studied her appraisingly, then he spoke.

"There are some things I need to know." He had thin lips and steely eyes.

"Yes, sir."

She was aware that the entire posse was listening, hushed and expectant. The only sound in the yard was the horses blowing through their nostrils.

The lieutenant said, "We're planning to search for Scott. I'm sure we'll find him quickly. But we need your help, Melissa. When did you last see him?"

"Ten o'clock. Last night. I was on the phone. He went out to the barn." She told the lieutenant about Mrs. Seliber's call.

"Then what did you do?"

"I took the roast from the freezer. I was going to go out to the barn, but it was so cold I decided to make Scott some hot chocolate instead."

"What happened then?"

"The light was on in the barn, so I thought Scott was okay."

"But he didn't come back."

"No," she said softly.

"Melissa, now this is important. How long was he gone?"

"Fifteen minutes."

"How do you know?"

"I looked at my watch. I remember thinking that fifteen minutes was a long time just to give Nosey a carrot. That's when I began to worry. I decided I'd better go to the barn."

"Why didn't you go after the boy sooner?"

"I don't know." Melissa's mouth was dry.

"Don't know." The lieutenant pursed his thin lips. Then

he said, "When you went out, did you see or hear anything unusual?"

"Well—earlier in the evening," Melissa said, "I thought I heard someone behind the barn."

The lieutenant and her father exchanged glances.

"But did you actually *see* anyone?" Lieutenant Krinn asked.

Melissa shook her head. The lieutenant made her feel like a criminal. She closed her eyes tightly and squeezed back the tears. She wouldn't cry in front of all these people. Especially Daniel.

"Okay." Lieutenant Krinn touched her arm. "That's it for now. I may have more questions later."

Addressing the posse the lieutenant said, "Riders, let's go over our plan once more. The Robinson house," he pointed over his shoulder, "is our command post. Detective Howard Price and I will man the phones and tape recorders in the house. We've divided the search pattern into four sectors—grids. Each grid is one square mile, about as equal as we can make 'em." He turned to his young, blond assistant. "Bring me the cardboard carton setting on the porch."

When the detective returned, the lieutenant began to draw in the snow with a stick. "You'll each work with a partner. Start with grid one—the forest preserve west trail bounded by Johnson's horse farm, Brown's house, the motel, and the river. Detective Price will give each of you one of these." The lieutenant patted the small black box attached to his belt. "It's a walkie-talkie. Communicate with your leader immediately if you find anything."

Price passed among them and distributed the walkie-talkies from the cardboard carton. "Press the button when you want to talk. Release the button and listen. The box is always on to receive. Got that?" he said. "Anyway, you won't be far apart."

Daniel cleared his throat. "What happens if we get out of range of the walkie-talkies?" His voice sounded husky, as if he had a cold.

"Contact the forest rangers cruising the area in cars. They'll be on the west trail too." said Lieutenant Krinn.

"When will the bloodhounds arrive?" asked Mr. Robinson.

"Should be soon. We've requested dogs from Boone County."

The lieutenant looked around the circle of faces. "Report back here at noon for lunch. We'll cover grid two this afternoon, grids three and four tomorrow. Hopefully we'll find Scott long before then. Any more questions?"

In the silence that followed, Melissa heard Butterball nicker at the hitching post.

"Good luck," Lieutenant Krinn said. He signaled Mr. Mansfield to get started.

"Riders—mount up with your partners," called her father.

When she was mounted Kory caught Melissa's eye and gave her a "thumbs up" sign.

Roscoe Cannon shouted from the rear. "Move 'em out!"

Melissa shuddered when she saw the grim look on Mr. Robinson's face as he rode out with the posse. She prayed they would find Scott—unharmed.

After the posse had gone, Melissa wished with all her heart that she was riding with them. If she couldn't ride with the posse, what else could she do to help find Scott? Search the barn again? Now that it was daylight, maybe, just maybe, there was a clue that she and Mr. Robinson had overlooked last night. It wasn't a brilliant idea, but it was the best she could come up with.

Melissa searched every nook and passageway in the barn, ducking filmy cobwebs laced in dark corners. Not a trace of Scott. The sweet, friendly smell of hay hit her nostrils and reminded her of the hayloft. There could be some clue hidden up there after all. She remembered the funny angle of the hay bale in the corner. Today the bale was gone.

Melissa felt shaky as she climbed the rickety ladder. She'd been up in the loft dozens of times, but since Scott was missing, all the familiar things seemed frightening.

Just as she was about to reach the top, there was a thud in the feed room below. The sudden sound caught Melissa off balance, and she almost fell to the floor. She grabbed the top rung of the ladder and managed to steady herself. "Who's there?" she called.

Another loud thud.

Melissa crawled into the loft. "Who's down there?" she shouted on her knees.

There were heavy footsteps on concrete. She caught her breath as the feed room door slowly creaked open. The familiar figure standing in the doorway, wearing worn jeans and cowboy hat, was Montana, the barn man.

"Missy!" he said. "Thought I heard someone. But filling the feed bins makes a heap of noise. What in holy Christmas are ya doin' up there?" Montana was an ex-cowboy with a ruddy face permanently creased by gusty winds.

"Oh, Montana," Melissa said as she backed down the ladder, "Am I glad to see you."

The barn man was around horses so much he gave off a strong horse odor. He stood in the aisle, twisting an empty feed bag in his work-roughened hands.

"Ain't it a stampede?" he asked. "About Scotty, I mean."

Montana had an odd way of expressing himself. Melissa knew that he meant it was awful that Scott was missing.

"He was only alone for fifteen minutes. Just fifteen minutes," she told him. Tears pushed into her eyes again.

Montana dropped the feed bag and put an arm around Melissa's shoulders. "Little fillies musn't cry over spilt milk." Montana was a little weird sometimes, but he liked kids.

Melissa sniffled. "I came to search the barn again."

"No use, Missy. Soon as there was a glimmer of light, Robinson and me searched the house and barn. Top to bottom. There was nuthin'." Montana picked up the feed bag, folded it neatly, and put in on a hay bale sitting in the aisle.

Hearing voices, Scott's horse stuck out her head and nickered.

"How's Nosey?" Melissa asked.

Montana shrugged. "Okay."

"What did Dr. Egel say?"

Montana wiped calloused palms on his jeans. "Uh— she's okay."

"But what did he say?" Melissa insisted.

"Didn't call the doc," Montana said.

"Why not?" Melissa felt uneasy. She'd never felt that way with Montana before.

"No need." The barn man slid open Nosey's stall. "Here, girl," he called. The little mare came to him. Montana hooked a lead rope to her halter and Nosey pranced into the center aisle.

"Full of vinegar, ain't she?"

"But Scott said she wouldn't eat," Melissa told him.

"Then a phantom must of got into her feed bin." He gave a little grin. "Licked it clean."

Was Montana telling the truth? When Melissa left the barn she wondered about that. She had always liked the barn man, but she didn't know much about him except that long ago, back home in Billings, he'd had a wife and a young son. At first she and Scott would ask him questions about the boy, but he seemed to go off in a haze and wouldn't answer. Lately they'd given up asking.

Montana was getting older and a little forgetful, but he was still strong, and he knew more about horses than anyone around. He'd been with the Robinson family for almost ten years, and Scott loved him. They were good buddies. Once Scott told Melissa that he wished Montana was his father.

Melissa scolded herself silently. You've no reason to be suspicious of Montana. If he didn't call the vet then Nosey didn't need a vet. And that was that.

The sound of a car approaching broke into Melissa's thoughts. A taxi pulled up, and the back door opened. Across the yard came Mrs. Seliber's booming voice, "Oh, I dropped the money in the snow. Sorry—I'm so upset. Our little boy is missing!"

Melissa watched as the housekeeper bent to retrieve the money. When the taxi drove off Mrs. Seliber, in knee-high boots, stamped up the back steps. It's all her fault, Melissa thought. If only she hadn't called about that stupid roast, Scott would be here right now.

As Melissa started for Butterball she heard Mrs. Seliber yell, "Melissa! Is that you—Melissa Mansfield?"

Her voice hurt Melissa's eardrums.

"It's me," Melissa said, walking back toward the porch where the housekeeper was standing.

"Any news about Scott? I came as soon as I got Mr. R.'s call."

"The posse is searching the woods. That's about all I know. Except that there are two policemen inside the house," Melissa told her.

"You shouldn't 've let him go to the barn alone that late.

Poor boy. Poor darling lad." Mrs. Seliber shook her finger at Melissa. "That was a mighty irresponsible thing to do, young lady."

That word "irresponsible" again!

Mrs. Seliber put the key in the door. After she went in, Melissa stood there feeling as if she'd been tarred and feathered and dragged through the streets by a horse. She'd seen it happen once to a bank robber in a TV movie special.

Melissa made a snowball and threw it against a tree. If only she could find Scott and show everyone that she was a responsible person. Where could he be? Think, she told herself. Think. She closed her eyes and searched her mind for the faintest clue—like Butterball cropping grass, choosing the juiciest shoots, rejecting the dry ones.

A memory raced by. Last summer, when Mrs. Seliber was on vacation, she and Scott had ridden to Lost Lake, deep in the woods. The only way to get there was on horseback or on foot. It was Scott's favorite place. Once, seeking shelter from the rain, they'd found a cave large enough for them and their horses in the hill overlooking the lake. Scott had thought it would be a neat place to hide. "You could hibernate here all winter—just like a bear," he had said, "And nobody would find you."

Melissa's eyes flew open. That was it!

Lost Lake!

She ran to the hitching post where Butterball was tethered.

On the way to Lost Lake, deer tracks in the snow were the only footprints Melissa saw. She kept on anyhow, figuring that Scott's trail had been erased by the new snow. It was rough going. Butterball took short steps, stamping down as he went, often sinking in up to his ankles where the snow was deepest. It was a good thing he had on winter shoes with borium cleats and pads covering his hooves so the snow wouldn't ball up.

Finally they worked their way to the cave. Melissa was so eager to get there she almost jumped off while Butterball was in motion. When she did dismount it took only a few moments to tether Butterball to a tree and run to the cave. She felt a pang of disappointment at seeing the huge drifts in front of the cave's entrance. Could they have been piled up by the wind after Scott hid inside last night?

"Scott!" she shouted, digging furiously at the drifts with her mittened hands. "Are you in there—you old bear?"

There was no sound except for Butterball pawing the snow. Finally she had dug an opening large enough for her to crawl through.

Inside the cave it was dark and damp and smelled of animal droppings. Melissa's hands and feet were wet and the dampness made her tremble. She wouldn't have minded the cold, if she had found Scott. And although she searched the entire cave, she knew it was empty the moment she came inside. In fact, she'd really lost hope of finding Scott here when she saw the high drifts outside the cave's entrance.

If Scott wasn't in the cave, where was he?

Coming out, Melissa blinked at the sundazzled view from the top of the hill. Everywhere the earth was thickened with soft, clean snow. Below, Melissa could see the winding road leading to the forest preserve, and the dark patches on the lake nestled in the valley where the water hadn't yet frozen. The snow-topped roof of the main house at the Boy Scout Camp looked as if it were layered with whipped cream.

Melissa barely noticed the beauty of the terrain. She was thinking of the day that she and Scott had eaten peanut butter sandwiches on the hill and pretended they had outlaws under surveillance on the road below, like Sheriff

John Wayne and his deputies did in a TV rerun. In a surprise attack she and Scott pretended to pounce on the bad guys, capture them, and tie them onto their saddles. Then, riding Nosey and Butterball, they loped off with the imaginary criminals to Sheriff Leonard's county jail.

Melissa sighed, and decided to go back to Scott's house. It was almost noon. Perhaps there would be some good news.

At the Robinsons' house, Melissa rang the back doorbell. While she waited, she peeked into the study window and saw Lieutenant Krinn and Detective Price seated behind a desk. They looked up briefly when they heard her on the porch.

Mrs. Seliber opened the door. "Well—Melissa."

"Hi, Mrs. Seliber, have you heard anything yet? From the posse, I mean."

"No," said the housekeeper.

"I've been searching for Scott, too. Up at Lost Lake." Melissa said.

"That wasn't smart—going so far alone. Leave that to the posse. You might get lost too. Then they'd have to look for both of you." She opened the door wider. "Come in. You look frozen."

The kitchen felt warm and cozy. Melissa took off her boots and left them on the mat near the door. Her fingers and toes began to tingle.

"I'm making lunch for the posse," Mrs. Seliber said.

Melissa threw her hat and jacket on a chair. She glanced at the delicious-looking rare roast beef, and her stomach growled. She hadn't eaten all day.

"How about a sandwich?" asked Mrs. Seliber.

Melissa sat on a kitchen stool. "Yes, please."

Hungrily, she bit into the sandwich. She heard the

lieutenant talking in the study, but the door was closed, and she couldn't make out what he was saying.

"Want some hot chocolate?" asked Mrs. Seliber.

The words "hot chocolate" hit Melissa like a punch in the stomach. They brought back last night's events as vividly as if they'd flashed on a large size TV screen. She'd made the drink for Scott last night in this very kitchen. At that stove. She'd let him go to the barn alone and he never came back. As hungry as she was, she couldn't swallow now.

Detective Price came into the kitchen and said to Mrs. Seliber, "Mansfield called. They're near the motel. End of grid one."

"Any news?" she asked eagerly.

"Nah. They'll be coming in soon. For lunch."

"All right," Mrs. Seliber said, her voice filled with disappointment. "I'll put on the coffee."

Melissa's stomach was tied in knots. When the house-keeper went into the pantry to get the coffee pot, Melissa put on her boots and jacket and called, "Thanks Mrs. Seliber, I'm leaving now."

As Melissa shut the door behind her, she heard the phone ring. She saw Lieutenant Krinn pick it up in the study. Melissa descended the stairs slowly. She had almost reached the bottom step when she heard a piercing scream. Terror crawled up her spine and covered her whole being. She turned, ran up the stairs two at a time. The housekeeper threw open the door and shouted, "Melissa! Scott's been kidnapped!"

CHAPTER 4

Saturday: Noon

Scott kidnapped!

Melissa's mind reeled. No! No, it isn't true. He can't be kidnapped. He just can't be. He was only gone for fifteen minutes!

"Lord! Oh, Lord!" boomed Mrs. Seliber, holding her head. She sank into a chair, her face pale.

The roar in Melissa's ears prompted her to hang on to the counter as the kitchen spun around her. A drink of water might have helped, but with legs like rubber bands she couldn't make it to the sink. Melissa dropped onto a stool. Her knees were shaking so hard she had to press them together.

Through the open study door, Melissa heard Lieutenant Krinn talking on the phone.

"We got a call," he was saying. "Just a few minutes ago. Male. Asked for Mike Robinson." He paused, and the refrigerator ice maker clinked loudly in the silence. "Said he'd call back," the lieutenant continued. "Said Robinson better be here if he wants to see his son again." Another pause. "Yep. Got it all on tape."

"Our poor little boy. Poor little Scott," Mrs. Seliber moaned over and over. "Just yesterday morning I baked him chocolate chip cookies. He stood right there." She pointed to the built-in ovens. "Couldn't wait for me to take them out." She began to sob—a hollow, whimpering sound that soon turned into a gushing torrent.

Mrs. Seliber's words added to Melissa's guilt, but the housekeeper's sobs shredded her nerves. This was worse than the time she had forced Butterball to cross a swollen river and had fallen in and almost drowned.

The crunch of hooves on crusty snow and horses nickering in the yard signaled the arrival of the posse. A few moments later, the entire group burst into the kitchen. Melissa felt the accusation in everyone's eyes.

She ran into her father's arms murmuring. "Oh Dad, I feel so awful." She wept tears hot with shame.

Her father held her tightly and stroked her hair. "Missy. Missy. Everything will work out. It has to."

She felt the scratchiness of his wool jacket on her chin, and her body began to relax.

Melissa stayed in the safety of her father's arms as the posse shouted questions and milled about Lieutenant Krinn. It was bedlam.

"Has Scott really been kidnapped?" "How do you know?" "Was there a phone call?" They peppered him with questions.

Mr. Robinson shoved his way in.

He shook the lieutenant's shoulder. "Is Scott all right? Is my boy alive?"

Lifting her head, Melissa saw Daniel Simcoe standing a few feet away, and knew that he'd been watching her. Why didn't he mind his own business? Sniffling, she reached for a tissue in her jacket pocket and blew her nose.

Lieutenant Krinn raised his arms in the air yelling above the noise, "All right. Quiet everybody! I'll tell you what I know."

As the kitchen quieted, Melissa saw Montana slip in the back door. Peering around the room, his face had a mournful, pushed-in look. But nobody else seemed to notice the barn man. Every eye in the room was on the lieutenant.

Lieutenant Krinn cleared his throat. "A guy called here about twenty minutes ago. We got him on tape. We'll play it for you."

The lieutenant motioned to the detective. Price walked over to the tape recorder on the kitchen table and turned it on.

The tape began, "Let me talk to Mike Robinson." It was only a hoarse whisper.

Then Lieutenant Krinn's voice said, "He's not here. Who is this?"

"Never mind," said the other voice. "Just tell Robinson that if he wants to see his son again—"

"Do you have Scott?" the lieutenant broke in.

The caller ignored the question and repeated, "If Robinson wants to see his son again, he'd better be at his phone at two o'clock this afternoon." There was a click—then the dial tone.

In the kitchen, nobody said a word until Mr. Robinson asked, "Is that all?"

"That's all," said the lieutenant, as Price rewound the tape.

"You couldn't trace the call?"

"No. He wasn't on long enough."

"And he didn't ask for ransom?"

"No. But ransom is probably the reason for the next call."

The lieutenant moved closer to Mr. Robinson. "By any chance, did you recognize the voice?"

Mike Robinson shook his head. "It's obviously disguised."

Lieutenant Krinn turned to the posse. "Does anyone recognize the voice?"

There was a small, gloomy silence, and the lieutenant cracked his knuckles.

Kory caught Melissa's eye and her face wrinkled with distaste.

When nobody spoke up the lieutenant said to the detective, "Price, play the tape again."

Melissa watched as Mr. Robinson listened intently, chewing his lip.

This time the voice sounded somewhat familiar to her. Was it because she'd already heard it on tape? It was hard to tell, it was so muffled. But it was rather nasal—as if the kidnapper had a cold or something.

When the tape was over, Mr. Robinson shook his head.

"I'm going to play it one more time," the lieutenant told him. "I know this is hard for you, but it's very important. Please concentrate."

When the tape concluded, Lieutenant Krinn said, "Is there anything—*any thing*," he divided his words for emphasis, "about the voice or what he said, that rings a bell?"

Mr. Robinson pursed his lips and looked up over his thick glasses.

"Someone you denied a loan at the bank? An ex-employee perhaps?"

"I can't place the voice—but . . ." Mr. Robinson's brow wrinkled in thought.

The lieutenant leaned forward. "But, what?"

"There is one little thing. I don't know if it means anything—but everyone at the bank calls me Mitchell. My real name."

"And this guy called you, 'Mike.'"

Mr. Robinson nodded. "Only my brother in California and my neighbors in Woodvale use that nickname. And I spoke to my brother at his home last night."

"Ummmm." Lieutenant Krinn digested the information, but he made no comment. He looked around at the posse and said, "We'll have to wait for the kidnapper's next call. Then I'll put a trap on to keep the line open, and our men will trace it and see where he's calling from."

Mr. Robinson nodded. Looking pale and shaken, he asked Mrs. Seliber for a cup of coffee.

"With a kidnapping, it's a whole new ball game," Lieutenant Krinn said.

"Will you call in the FBI?" Mr. Robinson asked, gulping his coffee.

"I'll have Price report the case to the FBI's computerized National Crime Information Center in Washington. Then we'll contact the hostage negotiation team. They'll get on the case immediately. After they trace the call via the trap, they'll dust for prints and question witnesses."

The posse members huddled together, talking softly.

"Posse," the lieutenant said getting their attention, "Since this case is now a kidnapping—we'll handle it from here on in with our own people. Thank you for your time this morning. You're excused."

Mr. Robinson stood up. "Friends—wait a minute. I . . ." he took a deep breath. "Thank you for helping." Then his voice broke. "Please have a bite of lunch before you go."

Red-eyed and sniffling, Mrs. Seliber brought out a tray of

cold meat and cheese and put it on the counter beside the coffee pot. Everyone began talking at once.

Melissa made herself a sandwich. Then, taking off her jacket and putting it on the back of a chair, she sat down at the kitchen table with Kory and the Brown twins.

"Coffee is just what I need," Kory said, gulping the hot liquid. "It sure was a long, cold ride."

"Yeah," said Allison, biting into her sandwich. "And nothing to show for it."

Kory took one look at Melissa's face and said, "I sure hope they find Scott."

"Me too," said Stacey.

Melissa couldn't eat. She pushed the sandwich around on her plate and stared across the kitchen. Daniel, in his navy blue jacket, was leaning against the bird-design wallpaper with his cowboy hat pulled down over his eyes. He had an intense, dark look on his face as he stared out the window.

All of a sudden he began to pound his chest and cough as if he couldn't breathe.

That's the fakest coughing spell I've ever seen, Melissa thought. Why is that beanpole pretending to be sick?

Kory asked her to pass the mustard, and when she looked back to where Daniel had been standing, he was gone. He'd left without eating a bite. If Daniel didn't eat, something was wrong. At school he always ate two sandwiches for lunch and pigged down two desserts.

Melissa thought about why Daniel might have left so suddenly. It wasn't too difficult to figure out. Scott's kidnapper had called Mr. Robinson Mike, not Mitchell. That meant he was either Mr. Robinson's brother, or one of the neighbors. Since the brother was in California last night around the time of the kidnapping, he couldn't have kidnapped Scott. So, the kidnapper had to be someone who lived in Woodvale.

Once on a TV mystery, the kidnapper was actually in the search party. He'd made the ransom call from a gas station during the search. Scott's kidnapper could be a member of the posse!

Melissa bit her lip. There were five men in the posse, besides Mr. Robinson—her father; Roscoe Cannon, his co-leader; Daniel; Dr. McCormack, Kory's father; and Mr. Johnson. Daniel's voice was hoarse. So was the voice on the tape. Melissa was getting excited. Could Daniel have made the call to Mr. Robinson? If so, where?

She went over every inch of the first grid in her mind. Slowly she pictured the forest preserve west trail bounded by Johnson's horse farm, then all the way down to Brown's house—there was no gas station in that part of the grid. She sighed.

The next boundry was the motel. *The motel!* There were pay phones in the lobby! Daniel could have made some excuse, gone in and called while his partner waited outside. Otherwise why was he in such a hurry to get away? Obviously to make the next phone call from home before the police put on the trap. It couldn't have been scripted better!

Melissa stood up and pushed back her chair.

"Where are you going?" Kory asked, squinting up at her. "You haven't touched your sandwich."

Kory always told Melissa that she jumped into things without thinking. How could she tell her friend that she was suspicious of Daniel when there wasn't one shred of evidence to back it up? Nobody, not even Kory, would believe her without proof.

"I've got a headache," she said, reaching for her jacket. "I'm going home."

Kory felt for the glasses on her nose. "It's no wonder

after all you've been through," she said sympathetically. "If you feel better later, come over. I rented a great movie."

"I'll try," Melissa said. "See you." She gave a little wave to the girls, zipped up her jacket and slipped out the back door.

She didn't need her sunglasses now. The day had started out sunny, but now the wind was edging up and the blue sky was covered by grayish-black clouds. It had begun snowing again. Melissa pulled her jacket collar tightly around her neck and started down the snowy path to the hitching post. There wasn't a minute to waste. She would have run all the way, but someone may have been looking out of the window, and she didn't want to attract attention.

She bridled Butterball, wiped the snow from her saddle with the sleeve of her jacket, and mounted quickly.

Where was Daniel likely to be? At his home, she thought. He'd probably be hanging around there until it was time to make the next phone call. She wanted to catch him at it. It wouldn't be easy to find him, though. He'd had a fifteen minute head start.

Gathering the reins, she signaled her horse to move out. Butterball tossed his head and pranced toward the back trail, his breath snorting smoke on the frosty air.

Melissa was always being told that she jumped into things without thinking, but this time it was different. She wasn't about to accuse the beanpole of anything until she had proof. Proof was what she was after now.

CHAPTER 5

Saturday, 1:00 P.M.

The back trail led past the Robinsons' barn where Scott's little red rocking horse, Happy, was sitting near the door. Melissa pictured the boy astride his horse, rocking back and forth, as he'd done for hours when he was younger. She remembered when Scott had outgrown his red horse, Mr. Robinson was going to give it to his small nephew in California, but Scott wouldn't part with it. He said he wanted his little horse to guard the barn forever. So Happy stayed.

"Happy, you must have seen the kidnapper," Melissa said aloud. "If only you could talk!"

She had to turn away from the intense black eyes reproaching her from under snowcapped brows. They seemed to say, "Why didn't you take better care of my friend?"

The latest dusting of wet snow on tree branches gave the trail an eerie cobweb-like aura. Melissa shuddered when she saw the Robinsons' horse trailer, like a prehistoric monster, with a huge snow dome atop its green plastic cover.

There was movement in the brush behind her, and Melissa stiffened. Quickly a furry rabbit hopped across the path and scurried out of sight. Sighing, she leaned back in the saddle.

She signaled Butterball into a slow canter. He threw his head, did a little sidestep, and then settled into an easy gait. While Butterball loped along the trail, occasionally jumping small logs that poked through the snow, Melissa thought about Daniel Simcoe again. Something was nagging at her. That something was motive. If Daniel Simcoe was involved in the kidnapping, what was his motive? I'm some detective, why didn't I think about that before? she asked herself.

She was nearing Daniel's house. At her approach, a variety of sparrows, blackbirds, jays, and cardinals, chattering on a large, wooden platform-type bird feeder, scattered into the nearby thicket. There wasn't time to figure out Daniel's motive now.

On a tall pole, near a clump of evergreens, there were at least a dozen feeders of various sizes and shapes hanging on pulleys. When she saw a tiny olive goldfinch clinging to a tube-shaped feeder, Melissa recalled Daniel's talk about birds in their science class last fall. How his eyes lit up when he told about outwitting the squirrels so they wouldn't eat the bird food. He used a metal dome hugging the pole she was looking at now. She remembered it well, because he'd shown photos and bragged about his bird "condo." The kids, including Melissa, had rolled their eyes and laughed at him, but Mrs. Decker said he was very creative and gave him an A.

Although bird lover didn't seem to be synonymous with kidnapper you could never tell. Melissa recalled a miniseries where the murderer raised chickens. Although he loved his baby chicks, he couldn't have cared less about his human victims.

Anyway, Melissa was here now, and she would shadow Daniel to get evidence. It was the first time she'd ever shadowed anyone, but she'd seen plenty of it done by TV detectives. Melissa knew the rules. Be as quiet as possible. And take care that your quarry doesn't spot you. Butterball must be tethered out of sight. She didn't want the Simcoes to know she was spying.

She slid to the ground. Leading the little palomino to the back of the barn, she used his reins to tie him to a tree stump. Melissa knew it wasn't a good idea to tie Butterball with the reins. A sudden lift of his head and they could easily be broken. But she didn't have time to halter and tie him properly with her lead rope. She rationalized that if she had to leave in a hurry, it would be easier to make a getaway.

Slowly but resolutely Melissa walked toward the barn. She felt a rising excitement. Was Daniel's horse there? She couldn't go inside for fear of stirring up a chorus of whinnies that would blow her cover. Rubbing a small circle with her glove on the frosted window pane, she peered in.

Although it had stopped snowing, she couldn't see a thing. She'd have to go inside after all.

The rusty hinges creaked as the barn door slowly slid open. Inside, the sweet smell of hay and apples mingled in the air with horseflesh.

Three horses peeked out through metal bars and squealed a welcome. But the empty stall in the corner meant that Socks, Daniel's sleek brown and white pinto, hadn't made it back here.

She was right! The beanpole wasn't sick. Then why did

he leave the Robinsons' so abruptly? And where was he now?

Closing the barn door behind her, Melissa looked over at the house. Crouching as low as possible, she crawled over the slippery redwood walk in that direction. The place was as deserted as the fairgrounds after a horse show. Now was the time to search for clues.

Melissa's heart hammered. She didn't want to be caught nosing around. If the beanpole was desperate enough to kidnap Scott, he could become violent.

She shouldn't have come here without thinking it through. Was this another of her irresponsible acts? Suddenly she felt chilled. And afraid. She'd better go back to the Robinsons' and tell the lieutenant about her suspicions. Pronto!

Just as Melissa got up, someone tackled her from behind. Her head snapped and her feet went flying from under her. She and her assailant fell on the snow with a thud that shook her to her teeth.

"Owwwwwwww!" she screamed.

The attack took her by surprise, but she was strong and quick and began fighting back. Her right hand clenched into a fist as she rolled over in the snow, punching the other person in the stomach. For a moment, they were a tangle of arms and legs. Then her attacker grasped her arms, threw her on her back, and pinned her to the snowy ground. Her legs thrashed out and kicked wildly.

Terrified, Melissa stared up into Daniel Simcoe's grim face. Her eyes were wide as she watched his gloved fist come threateningly close to her nose.

"Melissa Mansfield!" he said in a hoarse, surprised voice.

"I give up," she said meekly. "Let go."

His grip loosened and she sat up.

"What are you doing here?" he demanded.

"I came to wrestle," she said, struggling to her feet.

"Very funny," said Daniel.

Melissa brushed snow from the front of her jacket. Every bone in her body ached. She wanted to punch his crooked nose. But she knew that she was no match for him. The beanpole might be skinny, but he was strong. She'd have to outthink him.

He glared at her. "Why were you creeping around here?"

"I wasn't creeping."

Daniel grabbed her arm and she winced.

"You followed me here. Didn't you?" His voice was low. She didn't answer. She was afraid to.

"Why? Why did you follow me?" he repeated.

"Because I thought you knew something."

"I knew something?"

"About Scott's disappearance—I mean."

"Me? Scott? You thought . . ."

Melissa held her breath.

Daniel dropped her arm, threw his head back, and laughed. "You followed me because . . ." He laughed harder. This time it ended in a coughing spell. When he caught his breath he said, "You thought I was involved in the kidnapping?"

Still afraid, she rubbed her arm and gave a slight nod.

"We certainly are a pair of detectives," he said. "I know less about the kidnapping than you do. I left the posse early to nose around Roscoe Cannon's house. I thought he was acting strange."

"I was suspicious of you—your voice is raspy like the voice on the tape. . . ."

"I have a cold," Daniel said.

"And you didn't eat lunch."

"So you put two and two together and you got me."

"I guess so," she said meekly.

"Well, you were wrong. But I'm sorry about the pounding." He brushed snow from Melissa's collar. "When I saw this thing creeping around my house I . . . hey, you put up a pretty good fight," he said admiringly.

"Not good enough," Melissa said, still rubbing her arm.

"Truce?" he said. "You're not mad at me?"

She grinned and shook her head.

"Then come in and have a cup of coffee. You look frozen."

"Okay," she said.

When they entered the kitchen, Melissa sat down at the table and removed her jacket. Daniel made two mugs of instant coffee and set hers on a napkin.

"Want a doughnut?" he asked, rummaging in a cabinet and returning with a box of chocolate doughnuts.

"No, thanks." She took a sip of coffee and it warmed her insides.

"My folks are out of town for the weekend, and my sister and I are on our own—so there isn't much real food here."

"That's okay," said Melissa.

"Look," Daniel said, sitting down across from her. "I want to get to the bottom of this."

"Me too," she said. "Why do you suspect Roscoe Cannon? He's coleader of the posse. Lived next door to us for over five years."

"Yeah, he seems like a nice guy." Daniel bit into a doughnut. "But what do you *really* know about the man?"

She shrugged. "Not much. Keeps to himself mostly. He's a good rider. Got a wife and two small kids. I baby-sit for them sometimes."

He chewed thoughtfully. "Does he gamble?"

"Gamble?"

"You know—play poker. Go to Vegas."

"I don't know."

"Think. It's important."

"What's gambling have to do with Scott's disappearance?"

"Motive," Daniel said.

"Oh," said Melissa. "I see." But she didn't. She took another gulp of coffee and set the mug down.

"Money—or rather the lack of it—is a powerful motive for crime," Daniel said. "Does Roscoe have money problems?"

She shrugged. "How should I know? He always pays me. Why do you suspect Roscoe?"

"Well, Roscoe and I were partners during the search. He tried to get away from me. Twice."

"Are you sure?"

He coughed into a Kleenex. "Yep. The first time I came over he pretended he was just looking around. I figured out later he *was* looking around—for a phone."

"So?"

"So when we came to the motel . . ."

"At the end of grid one?"

Daniel nodded. "The horses were resting. Roscoe said he was freezing. Told me he was going in for a cup of coffee."

She wiped her mouth with the napkin. "Well, it sounds reasonable."

"But his face was sweating. And he looked back as if to see if I was following him. He called over his shoulder, 'Keep an eye on the horses. Okay? I'll be right out.'"

"Then what?"

"Nothing. Except he was in the motel long enough to make a phone call from the lobby. And it was just about the time the call came through at the Robinsons'."

She was disappointed. "That's pretty slim evidence."

"No slimmer than you suspecting me because of a raspy voice and not eating lunch."

Melissa felt her face flush.

"Besides, he came out another door, not the one near the coffee shop," Daniel continued. "I said I wished I'd had a cup of coffee. He stared at me—kind of disoriented. You'd think he'd never heard the word coffee before."

"So you decided to snoop around his house while he was having lunch at the Robinsons'."

"Right.. I was watching Cannon when Mike Robinson said nobody but his brother and the neighbors in Woodvale called him Mike. Cannon kept sweating and wiping his face. He looked guilty all right. Besides, he'd told me that his wife had taken his kids shopping, so the coast was clear."

She studied him closely. "What did you expect to find at Cannons'?"

"Maybe where he hid Scott last night."

Melissa admired the beanpole's detective work. He had a good head on those skinny shoulders. "Well, did you find anything?"

"Zilch. Before I could look around, Roscoe's wife and kids came back. I had to get away."

She stood up. "Maybe we should go there now. I know the layout of the place pretty well. It's a three bedroom ranch."

"Does it have a basement? Or an attic?"

"Uh uh."

"I don't think he'd hide Scott inside the house. Not with a wife and two kids around." He picked up the mugs and put them in the dishwasher.

Melissa nodded her head in agreement. Then something stirred in her mind. "Say, there's a little shack in the back of the barn where Mr. Cannon keeps extra bags of feed. He's the only one who goes there. It's a perfect place to hide a prisoner."

They stared at each other.

"Want to buzz over there now and look around before Cannon comes home?" Daniel asked.

"Sure. I live next door to him, so let's put the horses in our barn."

"Okay," said Daniel.

When the horses were locked in their stalls, Melissa and Daniel walked the shoveled path to the little shack in the woods in back of Roscoe Cannon's barn.

Melissa put her finger to her lips. "Shhh. Did you hear that?"

"It's only a crow," Daniel said. "Does Cannon keep the shack locked?"

"The door is always closed. But I don't think there's a lock on it."

"Well, it may be locked now."

"If it is, that should tell us something."

There was no lock on the door.

Daniel opened it easily, and Melissa and he looked around the little room. Fifty-pound bags of pellets, Omalene, and corn were stacked in three neat piles. And a snow blower was pushed into the corner. There was no room for anyone to hide a ten-year-old boy.

Melissa's disappointment showed. "I thought that maybe . . ."

Daniel patted her arm. "It was worth a try. Scott could have been kept here."

As they walked back to her house, Melissa realized that she no longer thought of Daniel as a beanpole. He had a logical mind, and seemed to be in control, something she was striving for. She remembered a TV program where two private eyes teamed up and shared information. Eventually they caught the criminal. Perhaps if she and Daniel put their heads together, they might solve this mystery. More than anything she wanted to find Scott and clear her reputation.

"Listen, Daniel," she said, "maybe we can team up. You know—work together. To find Scott."

It only took him a second to answer. "Why not? Two heads are always better than one." He grinned. "Unless they're on the same person."

"Wise guy," she said, laughing, and punched his shoulder.

He stuck out his hand. "Hi, partner."

They shook hands firmly.

"This could turn out to be the best partnership since the Lone Ranger and Tonto," he said.

"Enough jokes," Melissa said. "Let's get to work. Should we tail Cannon?"

Daniel groaned. "You sound like Nancy Drew."

She ignored his reference to the fictional girl detective. "Well, should we?"

He shook his head. "Too dangerous. First of all, we're not sure he's the kidnapper. But if he is—he's a tough customer. Too tough for us to handle alone."

Melissa thought about what Daniel said. "Then I'm for going back to the Robinsons' to see what we can find out."

"Okay. Mike should have gotten the second phone call by now."

All was quiet when Melissa and Daniel rode into the Robinsons' yard.

"See anyone?" Melissa asked, trying Butterball to the hitching post.

"It's like a desert island."

Melissa hunched her shoulders inside her jacket. "More like the North Pole."

When they reached the porch Daniel said, "Maybe Mrs. Seliber will clue us in."

"Mrs. Seliber hates me."

"Man, you sure have a low opinion of yourself."

"She thinks Scott's disappearance is all my fault. Everyone does. Even my parents."

"Well, I don't. I think the kidnapper would have taken him sooner or later—no matter who was taking care of Scott."

His words made Melissa feel better. "Let's go right up and ring the bell," she said.

The housekeeper answered their ring, her eyes red and more swollen than before. "Oh, Melissa," she said, "go away."

"Please, Mrs. Seliber . . ." Melissa stuck her boot in the door.

"We've got enough trouble without you kids hanging around," she said, blowing her nose.

Melissa stepped closer and said softly, "Just tell me this—did the kidnapper call again?"

The housekeeper threw a scared look behind her.

"Please. I'm so worried about Scott," Melissa urged.

Mrs. Seliber lowered her voice to what was for her a whisper. "He wants $50,000!"

Melissa gasped.

"That's a lot of money," Daniel said. "Did the police trace the call?"

"They tried to. But he hung up too fast." Mrs. Seliber shook her head. "Poor Mr. R. The kidnapper made him promise not to bring the police. But he shouldn't go out to Lost Lake alone."

"Lost Lake!" Melissa turned to Daniel. "I've been there lots of times—even went there this morning."

"It'll be pitch dark at eleven o'clock," said Mrs. Seliber. "He could be murdered. And Scott too."

"Is Robinson supposed to leave the money at eleven o'clock tonight?" Daniel asked.

Mrs. Seliber nodded. "The kidnapper said that if the police set a trap for him we'd never see Scott again!" Then she stepped back. "I talk too much." Shaking a stubby forefinger at them she said, "You two better leave. And don't tell anyone what I told you."

As soon as the door slammed behind Mrs. Seliber, Melissa said, "We've got to stake out Lost Lake."

"Stake out?" Daniel asked. "Did anyone ever tell you that you watch too much TV?"

Melissa tossed her head, and started down the stairs. "You know what I mean."

As they walked toward their horses, Butterball whinnied and Socks joined in with a nicker. Melissa patted the palomino's neck absentmindedly. She was hatching something, and she hoped Daniel would go along with her idea. "Listen, there's a secret cave on a narrow trail above Lost Lake," she told him. "It's big enough for us and our horses. We could hide there."

He looked at her quizzically. "Why would we hide there?"

"To have a good view of the road below."

"Okay. Suppose we hide there. Then what?"

"Mr. Robinson leaves the ransom money, but doesn't know we're there. We wait. When the kidnapper picks it up later—we nab him!" she said triumphantly.

"Oh, sure. We see this dangerous criminal and we knock him out. With what? A snowball?" Daniel made a throwing motion. "Gotcha!"

"Daniel! Be serious."

"*You* be serious. Do you know that kidnapping is a federal

crime? We're no match for a real criminal. He could have a gun!"

Feeling stupid, Melissa drew the reins over Butterball's head, preparing to mount. "Guess I'm not being realistic," she said.

"No wonder you get into so much trouble."

Melissa flinched. Yet, as they rode out of the yard, she had to admit that Daniel was right. It wasn't smart for two kids to try to capture a desperate criminal.

As they jogged along, Melissa had a new thought. Daniel and she could ride their horses to Lost Lake, hide in the cave, and watch the road from above. When the kidnapper came, they'd be able to identify him. Then they could ride back to the Robinsons' place and tell the police.

She told Daniel her new plan.

He still wasn't convinced. "It's pretty dark at eleven o'clock. We have to be able to identify the kidnapper. How would we see his face if we're way up in some kind of cave?"

"There's a full moon tonight. And I'll bring my binoculars."

"Even with a full moon, all you'll be able to see is the top of his head."

"Well," she said, and her mind raced, searching for a new idea. "Okay—how's this for a retake? We wait in the cave until we see where Mr. Robinson puts the ransom money. Then we leave the horses up there and go below, closer to the road, and watch for the kidnapper. There are lots of trees and rocks to hide behind."

Daniel didn't even have to think about it. "Now that makes sense," he said. "But we'll have to go there real early."

"I'll meet you at nine o'clock. At the entrance to the trail leading to Lost Lake." She told him how to get there.

As they jogged toward her house, Melissa said, "My only problem now is how to sneak out tonight without my parents knowing."

"A piece of cake for me," Daniel said. "When mom and dad are out of town, my sister never bothers with bed check."

"It won't be easy for me," Melissa said. "But I'll think of something."

CHAPTER 6

Saturday Evening

The entire conversation at dinner that evening was about the kidnapping. As her parents talked, Melissa fiddled nervously with the pepper shaker.

"How will Mike raise fifty thousand dollars on a weekend?" Connie Mansfield asked her husband.

"No problem," said Mr. Mansfield. "He arranged it late this afternoon with the officers of his bank."

"Well, it's not smart for him to go out to Lost Lake alone—especially with all that money." Anxiety was showing all over her mother's face. "Why don't the police follow him?"

"The kidnapper made it clear that he was to go alone," said her father. "He has no choice."

"Maybe the bank marked the money, or something," Melissa put in. "They do it in TV kidnappings—so they can trace it."

Mrs. Mansfield sighed. "I wish this was one of your make-believe TV detective stories, Missy."

"I wish it was too," said her dad, "but we heard the kidnapper on tape. He's real all right."

Her mother stirred some sugar in her tea. "Chuck, do you think it's anyone in Woodvale? Someone we know?"

Melissa squirmed in her chair.

"I don't know." Her father stood up. "Guess I'm too tired to think. Up at dawn—organizing the posse—riding for hours in the cold." He brought his plate to the sink. "All this excitement, and trying to help Mike . . . I'm beat." He rinsed his plate and put it in the dishwasher.

"Honey, why don't we make a fire in our bedroom, and watch TV tonight instead of going out?" Mrs. Mansfield said.

"Good idea!" Mr. Mansfield smiled at her gratefully. "I have a few reports to go over. Then we'll hit the sack."

Melissa's heart fell. She had hoped her parents were going out as they usually did on Saturday night. It would have made it easier for her to get away. She'd planned to plump up her pillow, and pull the covers up. In the dark, they'd think she was asleep if they looked in.

She began to clear the table. Well, she still had two hours before she was to meet Daniel. Hopefully she'd be able to figure out a new plan.

It was almost eight-thirty when she heard her parents come upstairs. Melissa was in bed. She had on her plaid bathrobe over her blue jeans, presumably reading a book. But she was just turning pages when the phone on her nightstand rang.

"It's me," Daniel said. "What's happening?"

"Nothing." She kept her voice low. "They're staying home tonight."

"Think you can get out?"

"I hope so."

"Make it soon. We don't have much time."

"Okay," she whispered.

Just as she hung up the phone rang again.

"So, how's your headache?" Kory asked.

"Uh—not too good. I'm in bed."

"I thought it would be gone by now." Kory sounded disappointed. "All the kids are coming over. We rented this terrific movie, and we're sending out for pizza."

Ordinarily Melissa would have jumped at the invitation, but not tonight. Not when she was going to a stake out at Lost Lake.

"Thanks a bunch, Kory, but I don't feel up to it. Call you tomorrow. Okay?"

"Well, all right. Feel better."

As Melissa said good-bye there was a knock at her door and her mother said, "Missy?"

"Come in, Mom."

Her mother looked tired. There were lines around her eyes that Melissa hadn't noticed before.

"Oh, you in bed already Missy?" she said.

"Just reading."

"Thought I heard you talking on the phone."

"Kory called. She's having some kids over. She wanted me to come—but I'm beat."

Mrs. Mansfield bent over and kissed Melissa's forehead. "It's been a long day. A very long day. Dad and I are weary too."

Melissa avoided her mother's eyes. "I'll just read another chapter and turn out the light."

"Not staying up for the Perry Mason movie?"

"Uh uh."

"You must be tired." Mrs. Mansfield said, pulling the belt of her robe tighter around her slim waist. "Well, try to get some sleep."

She turned when she got to the door, "Scott will probably be home when you wake up. Then it'll all be over."

Melissa sighed. "I sure hope so, Mom."

As soon as the door closed behind her mother, Melissa jumped out of bed and threw her robe on a chair. Quickly, she pulled on her heavy woolen socks and boots. She'd even brought her jacket upstairs so she wouldn't have to search for it downstairs in the dark.

Melissa's heart hammered as she opened the door to the hall. Slowly she crept down the stairs. Would they hear her? The shower was running and their TV was on. She'd never done anything like this before. But if she told her parents what she was about to do, they'd never let her go.

Melissa was almost downstairs. At the last moment she remembered not to put her full weight on the second stair from the bottom—it always creaked loudly.

She'd made it! Melissa sighed in relief. No time to waste. She stuffed a couple of apples into her pocket, grabbed a flashlight, and ran out the back door. She was careful to leave the latch open so she could return.

With only the flashlight's beam to light the aisle, Melissa saddled Butterball. Although her parents' bedroom faced the front of the house and the barn was in the back, she didn't want to turn on the barn lights.

Working fast, she hooked Butterball's bridle, tightened the cinch under his belly, and led him outside to the mounting block.

All at once a piercing nicker split the night air. Melissa stopped in her tracks. It was Stormy! Once again her dad's horse called loudly to Butterball. Tying the reins over the hitching post, she quickly ran back to the barn and threw a few flakes of hay in Stormy's stall. Instantly his head went down and he began munching. He wouldn't miss his barnmate now.

Melissa mounted her horse and started down the moonlit trail. *Brrr*, it was cold. She pulled her wool hat down over her ears. She had often taken Butterball on moonlight rides—but never in this kind of weather. Suddenly, a night cloud sped by pushed by the wind, and it blocked the moon. In the darkness, fear crept into Melissa's throat. Despite the cold, she was sweating. Butterball felt her fear. He planted his feet and wouldn't budge.

Melissa reached down, patted her horse's neck and spoke softly to him. "C'mon boy. Don't be afraid. It's only a cloud. It'll be light again soon." At her nudging, Butterball moved forward slowly.

As they walked along in the darkness, Melissa felt a shiver up her spine. She was having second thoughts about being on that scary trail alone. What girl in her right mind would sneak out of a warm house on a freezing January night, and ride miles in the dark, to stake out a kidnapper? Kory wouldn't. Despite all the TV stories Melissa had watched, what did she really know about catching a desperate criminal?

A light shone ahead where she was to meet Daniel. Melissa was relieved to see him. The horses whinnied to each other, and Melissa signaled her arrival with her flashlight. There was no turning back now.

"You're late," Daniel said impatiently.

Melissa flashed the light on her Timex. Nine-thirty.

"Well, at least I'm here," she said.

"Let's get to the cave," he said. "You lead."

Ducking a low branch, Melissa took off down the narrow trail with Daniel following closely behind her. They didn't talk much during the half hour it took to get there.

When they arrived, the full moon shone again through the trees, dappling the ice-patched lake below with moonlight. Mr. Robinson wasn't due for a while. Melissa dismounted, and led Butterball toward the cave. When he passed Socks, the two horses sniffed and nuzzled one another. Since Butterball was used to the cave he went in willingly, but Socks snorted and refused to move. Butterball nickered to him. He took a few hesitant steps and looked around. Then he took another cautious look. Finally, he went inside. Soon both horses were asleep standing up, locking their leg joints to keep their legs from buckling.

Melissa took binoculars from her saddle bag and surveyed the road below. All was quiet.

She went inside again, and she and Daniel huddled together near the mouth of the cave on an old blanket that Melissa had brought along.

Daniel offered her a little bag of seeds.

"What's this?" she asked. "Some of your birdseed?"

Daniel threw his head back and laughed. He had nice teeth—a nice laugh too. "Close. It's sunflower seeds."

"When you're with a bird lover, who knows what he'll feed you," Melissa said, smiling. "Seriously though Daniel, your bird condo is awesome."

"How did you know I called it my condo?"

She bit into a sunflower seed. "From your talk in science."

"So you were the one," he said, grinning.

"What do you mean?" she asked, chewing the seed.

"The one who didn't fall asleep during my talk."

"Oh, Daniel. You're too much."

"No foolin'. Everyone seemed bored. They're always bored when I talk."

"That's not true." Melissa took a handful of seeds this time. "You're not boring at all. In fact, you're a . . . very interesting person."

"Did my mom pay you to say that?"

She giggled. Daniel had a great sense of humor, and he

was not the least bit boring. She encouraged him to tell her about his other hobbies. Besides liking birds and horses he played basketball and chess.

Daniel proved to be a good listener too. Melissa found herself pouring her troubles into his sympathetic ears.

When she stopped talking he said, "Why are you always putting yourself down? You have lots of good qualities."

Was he joking?

"Name one," she challenged.

"I can think of several off the top of my head," he said. "You have courage—didn't you come creeping around my house when you thought I was guilty?"

When she laughed and waved her hand at him, he said, "Don't laugh. You're persevering too," he continued. "You won't give up looking for Scott."

It was neat to have someone on her side for a change.

"Speaking of courage," he said, "Man, I'm the one that's chicken. I've never had the guts to talk to you at school."

Melissa didn't say anything, because she didn't know what to say. In the silence, she could hear the rhythmic breathing of the horses behind them in the cave.

She glanced at Daniel sidewise. Was he trying to tell her that he liked her? With the moon lighting his face he looked serious. All she could think of to say was, "I'm glad we're friends now." Not too brilliant, but the horses began to stir, and she didn't have to say anything more. Someone was coming on the trail down below.

Daniel put his finger to his lips. Then he stood up and went out. Melissa was right behind. They crouched behind a tree, waiting, barely daring to breathe. In the bright moonlight, looking through her binoculars, Melissa recognized Mike Robinson's horse, Fever. The big Thoroughbred snorted loudly, threw his head, and pranced up to the largest willow tree on the north side of the lake.

Mr. Robinson promptly dismounted. Holding on to the horse's reins, he looked around as if to see if anyone was watching. Then he reached up into his saddle bag and took out a package. Bending over, he placed the package at the foot of the willow. Then without looking right or left, he mounted again and galloped away.

It all happened so fast. Melissa couldn't believe the ransom money was placed there for the kidnapper and Mr. Robinson had gone. Now there was nothing for them to do but creep down the hill closer to the willow and wait.

"Let's go down now," said Melissa.

"I've been thinking," Daniel said, "if we lead the horses down and tie them in those trees," he pointed to a clump of evergreens below, "we won't have to climb up the hill again later to get them."

"Okay," Melissa said. "We'll take them now."

They returned to the cave and woke the horses. At first Butterball didn't want to leave, but Melissa tugged on the reins and he soon followed her down the hill.

"This is slow going in the dark," Melissa said. "Slippery too."

"Take it easy," warned Daniel. "Watch those deep drifts."

Step by step they went down, alert for the sound of a horse approaching.

"Hope the kidnapper doesn't get there before us," Melissa said.

At that moment, there was a rustle in the brush below.

Melissa stiffened, and pulled her horse's reins.

"Someone is in those bushes," she whispered.

Daniel stopped Socks, and cupped his ear.

It was a scratching sound—like fingernails on tree bark.

"Ugggh," said Melissa, in a low voice. "That goes right through me."

"Shhhh," Daniel said, "I'm trying to listen."

There was a long, terrifying hiss, and out in front of them jumped a plump racoon—then another, racing after.

"Wow!" said Melissa. "Racoons are sure scary in the dark."

"You bet!" Daniel said. "But they're long gone now."

Melissa and Daniel started down again.

Finally they reached the evergreens, and Daniel said, "This is where we'll tie the horses. They can't be seen from the road."

"Okay," Melissa said. "Let's hide behind that big boulder. We'll have a good view of the big willow where Mr. Robinson left the ransom money."

This was the most dangerous stage—waiting for someone to ride out of the shadows to the appointed spot.

The next hour seemed endless to Melissa. She had gone out and peered at the road dozens of times. There was nobody in sight. She was freezing. Her back and legs ached. Taking off her gloves, she blew on her fingers. Like her toes, they were absolutely numb.

Melissa flashed the light on her Timex again. Midnight. They'd been out there for over two hours. Time stretched cold and silent. Yet, she had the uneasy feeling that something was about to happen.

A sudden weird scream pierced the air. It sounded almost human. The horses wakened and whinnied softly. Melissa went over and patted Butterball to calm him, while her own heart pounded. Something was out there. Something terrifying.

"What's that?" she whispered, her voice trembling.

Then there were eight loud hoots: whoo, whoo, whoo,

whoo, whoo, whoo, whoo, whoo-ah. Each one sent a tremor through Melissa from her toes to her scalp.

"Just an old hoot owl," said Daniel.

"He scared me," Melissa said.

Daniel put his arm around her and drew her close. She sighed, and leaned against him, feeling safe.

She stayed there until Butterball began to nicker and paw the snow.

"He hears something," Melissa said. For the umpteenth time she peeked out and looked at the road through her binoculars.

Nothing.

"Socks is pawing, too," Daniel said, standing beside her. His voice was low and taut.

"Dad says horses see with their ears," Melissa said. "They know someone is coming. Even if we can't see or hear him."

"Hope they don't give us away," Daniel said. "Just when we're about to identify the kidnapper."

Daniel patted and soothed Butterball again, assuring the little palomino that all was well. He gave each of the horses one of the apples Melissa had brought, and they soon quieted.

Daniel and Melissa took up their stance behind the boulder again. The next time Melissa looked out, her heart quickened when, through her binoculars, she saw a shadowy figure approaching on horseback. The kidnapper was coming to the appointed spot, using more caution than a horse approaching an electric fence. She strained her eyes, willing them to identify the rider.

"Who is it?" Daniel whispered.

"Someone on horseback."

"I know that! But who?"

"I can't tell yet."

Daniel made an impatient sound. "Give me the binoculars," he said, stretching out his hand.

He adjusted the glasses to his eyes. "Still too far away," he said. "Here, take 'em back."

Melissa riveted the binoculars on the distant figure.

Clouds scurried over the full moon. When it was light again, Daniel said, "See his face now?"

"No. He's still not close enough—he's taking his time getting there—looking around a lot."

"Probably making sure the police aren't watching."

She nodded. "Now he's rounding the bend and coming along the lake shore." Her voice was edged with excitement.

Finally the shadowy figure rode into full view.

"Quick, tell me," whispered Daniel. "Is it Cannon?"

She shook her head. Hard as she tried, it was impossible for Melissa to identify the rider. A long, black poncho fully covered him and his horse.

CHAPTER 7

Sunday—Early Morning

"It's the kidnapper all right," Melissa told Daniel. "He's heading straight for the willow tree!"

It was so quiet she could hear her heart beating.

"What's he doing now?" Daniel asked.

"Shhh. Sounds carry at night," Melissa cautioned. "If he thinks someone is watching, he might be so angry that he'd want to hurt Scott."

"Well, what's he doing?" Daniel whispered.

She peered through the glasses. "Dismounting."

"Do you recognize the horse?"

"No. He tied it behind a clump of trees. The guy is on his knees near the big willow now."

"What's taking so long?"

"He can't seem to find the ransom."

The kidnapper momentarily snapped on his flashlight. Startled, his horse bounced from behind the trees. In that split second the horse and the man's face were plainly visible to Daniel and Melissa, even without binoculars.

They faced each other and whispered in unison, "Roscoe Cannon!"

Then they stood rooted as Cannon mounted his horse, melted into a shadow and disappeared. Melissa's heart was thumping. One minute he was kneeling on the ground, the next he had grabbed the money—and then he was gone!

"What are we waiting for?" Daniel asked. "Let's go!"

As Daniel and Melissa untied their horses and mounted, a loud splash broke the night's stillness. Something had fallen into the water, but there was no time to investigate now.

Melissa slid her feet into the stirrups, gathered the reins in gloved hands and wheeled Butterball after Daniel. She wanted to kick her horse into a fast canter, but Daniel pointed out that if they overtook Cannon he'd know that they'd been spying on him.

"Be patient, Melissa," he said. "Remember our agreement? To alert the police after we've identified the kidnapper? They are the ones who'll find the ransom money on him. And they are the ones who'll capture him. Not us. Got that?"

She'd almost blown it! Thank goodness Daniel was here to keep her from acting without thinking. That very thing had happened in a mystery on TV once, when a private eye had loused up the metro police's coverup, and everyone was back to square one in finding the kidnapper.

They trotted down the snowy path, keeping a sharp eye ahead for Cannon. Melissa's tension mounted. She couldn't wait to tell Mike Robinson and Lieutenant Krinn what they had seen.

Later, in the Robinsons' family room, Lieutenant Krinn stared at Melissa and Daniel. "Now slow down, please. Let me get this straight. You kids actually saw the kidnapper pick up the ransom?"

Melissa and Daniel nodded vigorously.

"Describe the location of the money drop," said Lieutenant Krinn.

"It was a tree, near the lake," said Melissa.

"What kind of tree?"

"A big willow—the biggest around."

"And what side of the lake was it on?" the lieutenant asked Daniel.

"The north side," Daniel said.

Mr. Robinson, looking gaunt in a dark red cashmere robe, fingered his stubbled chin. "That's the place all right."

"Now," said Lieutenant Krinn, "tell me again, Melissa. You can *positively* identify Roscoe Cannon as the man who picked up the money?"

She sent a triumphant glance to Daniel. "Positively."

"It was midnight. Very dark. How could you be so sure?" the lieutenant said.

"The moon was full. Besides, he turned on his flashlight."

Mr. Robinson shook his head. "It can't be Cannon. We've been neighbors and friends for years. He's got two kids of his own."

"It was Roscoe Cannon," said Melissa stubbornly.

"But how could he have made the first phone call? He was riding with the posse," said Mr. Robinson.

Melissa nodded to Daniel and he told about Cannon going into the motel.

Mr. Robinson was still not convinced. "I don't understand. I've never done anything to harm Cannon or his family. Why would he kidnap Scott?"

The lieutenant cracked his knuckles. "People do strange things for money." He turned to Melissa and Daniel. "My men were going to be hidden in the woods. At first we planned an ambush at the ransom drop. But it was too risky." He pursed his lips. "We may have captured the kidnapper, but if there was a gunfight—he could have been killed before he told us where he'd hidden the boy."

At the word gunfight, Melissa's eyes found Daniel's. How lucky we were, she thought, that nobody was hurt.

"So," continued the lieutenant, "we put a beeper on the money and hoped to trace the guilty party that way. The signal was clear until just after midnight. Then we lost it . . ."

"We heard a splash when Roscoe rode out," Daniel broke in. "He must have thrown the beeper into the lake."

"Crafty guy. Probably heard us talking about it," Lieutenant Krinn said. "But thanks to you two we've got the goods on him anyway." He nodded to Mr. Robinson. "We'll put him away for a long time."

"I want my boy back safe and sound. That's all I care about," Mike Robinson said. "What are you going to do now, lieutenant?"

"I've contacted my men. As soon as they get here we'll surround Cannon's house. Since there's not much he can do with the ransom until tomorrow, he's probably in bed right now. Anyway, the money is marked."

"I'm going with you," said Mr. Robinson. He hurried upstairs to get dressed.

Melissa wished she and Daniel could go too. For a moment she had the wild idea of hiding out in the woods in back of Roscoe's house to watch the capture, but the lieutenant signaled Price. "It's late. Follow the kids in your car. See that they get home safely with their horses." He smiled at Melissa and Daniel. "Good work, guys."

As Melissa and Daniel rode out into the frosty night, they saw the unmarked police cars silently pulling into the yard.

It seemed as if Melissa had just slipped into bed and closed her eyes when someone was shaking her shoulder.

"Missy! Wake up!" Her mother, dressed in the familiar peach velour robe, was standing there.

Melissa sat up and rubbed her eyes. "What time is it?"

"It's morning—barely. Lieutenant Krinn called. Seems they've been up all night. They've got a suspect they want you to identify. At the Robinsons'."

Mrs. Mansfield handed Melissa her slippers. "What suspect? Why you? What's going on?"

Melissa was wide awake now remembering the stake out and identifying Cannon last evening. "Did they find Scott?"

"No." Mrs. Mansfield sat on the edge of the bed while Melissa put on her slippers. "That's the first thing I asked the lieutenant."

Melissa's heart sank. "They didn't find Scott?" Impossible. She's seen Cannon pick up the ransom money with her own eyes. What could have happened?

"Who is the suspect the lieutenant is talking about?" her mother asked again.

While Melissa washed and dressed, she told her mother what had happened while she and Daniel were staked out the night before.

"You what?" Her mother's eyes opened wide. "You left this house and were out practically all night? With Daniel Simcoe?"

"Aw, Mom. I came home a little after midnight." She grinned. "With police escort."

"You might have been killed!"

"Well, I wasn't. Anyway, they've got Cannon now."

Her mother's cheeks grew red. "Dammit, Melissa, you're so—irresponsible I just can't handle it anymore. Running out at night when we thought you were in bed . . ."

She knew her mom would blast her for it and she didn't

blame her. But this was no time for a lecture. "Please, Mom. Not now. I've got to get over to the Robinsons'."

"I won't forget about this, young lady. But okay—we'll deal with it later."

She'll probably ground me for a month, Melissa thought. Well, guess I deserve it.

Her mother sighed and shook her head. "Grab something to eat before you go, Missy."

But Melissa wasn't hungry. She hadn't been since Scott had disappeared.

Daylight was beginning to glimmer when Melissa rode Butterball into the Robinsons' yard. The unmarked police cars she'd seen pulling in the previous night were parked in the yard, and Socks was tethered to the rail in front of the barn. She tied Butterball there too, and the horses sniffed each other and squealed noisily in greeting.

A subdued Mrs. Seliber led Melissa into the family room, where Lieutenant Krinn paced up and back in front of the blazing fire, cracking his knuckles. Pen in hand, one of the detectives was behind a desk ready to take notes. Detective Price was seated next to him. Two other detectives were present, too. Daniel, slouching on the leather sofa, smiled a welcome and promptly had a coughing spell.

Melissa sat down on the sofa beside Daniel. Looking from face to face she zeroed in on Mr. Robinson. Tiredness showed in dark smudges under his eyes as he stood staring at Roscoe Cannon.

Cannon, although bearded, had thinning hair that he combed from one side to the other. There were deep creases in his forehead, and his rounded cheeks ended in a plump, oval chin. Bushy eyebrows accented his protruding brown eyes, making him look somewhat sinister. Yet Melissa had never thought of him in that way before. When he walked her home after baby-sitting, he'd never been very friendly toward her, like some of the other neighborhood men. Now he scowled at Melissa from the leather lounge chair where he was seated.

Lieutenant Krinn cleared his throat. "Okay. We've read you your rights, Cannon, and you've agreed to answer our questions voluntarily." He nodded to the detective at the desk and said, "Make a note of that."

"I've got nothing to hide," said Cannon.

"We'll see about that," said the lieutenant. "You say you were home last evening. Never left the house. Right, Cannon?"

"Yes, sir," he said crisply.

Melissa traded looks with Daniel.

"And you've never seen this pouch containing fifty thousand dollars—the ransom money?"

"That's correct," said Cannon.

"How come we found it buried in the woods in back of your property?"

"I don't know."

The lieutenant looked him in the eye. "Why would it be on *your* property?"

Cannon shrugged. "It's woods. Anyone could have hidden it there."

"Did you?"

He met the lieutenant's look. "No."

A wave of anger swept over Melissa. Why that miserable lying buzzard, she thought.

"Okay, Melissa. Tell Roscoe Cannon here what you and Daniel Simcoe saw last night," said the lieutenant.

Melissa felt all eyes on her. Her knees began to shake. "Well—last night—about ten o'clock, Daniel and I . . ." She looked at Daniel who nodded as if to back up what she was going to say. "Daniel and I," she repeated, "hid out in a cave on a bluff above Lost Lake. At eleven we saw Mr.

Robinson leave a package near the big willow tree. On the north side of the lake." She stopped and took a deep breath. "Afterward, we crept down, hid behind a boulder, and kept a watch on the place where he'd left the money."

Melissa looked around the room. Then, her voice an octave higher, "About midnight, we saw Roscoe Cannon in a black poncho pick up the pouch with the money."

Cannon jumped up as if he had been kicked by a horse. "It's a lie!" He pointed his finger at Melissa. "She's to blame for the kidnapping." He turned to the lieutenant. "She's trying to save her own skin."

Melissa's eyes blazed. "That's not true!"

"It was dark," the lieutenant said to Melissa. "Are you sure you can positively identify this man as the person you saw at Lost Lake?"

She faced Cannon. "Positively. I saw him through my binoculars."

"Binoculars!" Cannon gave a little laugh. "That's a good one."

"And you, Daniel?" said the lieutenant. "Any corrections or additions?"

"Well, Melissa had binoculars. But you didn't need them. There was a full moon, and when Cannon flashed his light on, I definitely saw him and his horse," he said.

"It wasn't me," protested Cannon. "I was home in bed."

"Do you have a witness to back up your alibi?"

"My wife will vouch for me."

How awful, Melissa thought. Our word against theirs.

"Listen, Cannon," the lieutenant said, "we know you're lying." He held up the ransom pouch once again. "We found your fingerprints all over this pouch."

There was a moment of silence.

Cannon jumped up. His eyes darted around the room like

a horse with his foot caught in barbed wire. "You didn't," he screamed. "I was wearing gloves!"

When Cannon realized that he'd admitted picking up the pouch, his body crumpled. He sank back into the chair and seemed to wilt before their eyes.

"I'll ask you once more, Cannon," said Lieutenant Krinn. "Have you ever seen this money pouch before?"

Cannon's face had a vacant look. He was pale, his hands were shaking, and his lips were pressed together. He didn't answer.

"Speak up, man," ordered the lieutenant.

When Cannon said, "Yes," it was barely audible. He turned to Mr. Robinson and pleaded, "Mike, forgive me. I was desperate! I owed so much money—gambling debts. To real gangsters."

"So you thought kidnapping a rich kid was the answer to all your problems?" said the lieutenant.

"They were going to kill me!" Cannon cried.

The lieutenant said to Mr. Robinson, "There's the motive all right."

His face rigid with fury, Mr. Robinson leaped over and grabbed Cannon by the throat. "*I'm* going to kill you! Where is my boy?"

The two detectives who were standing near the paneled wall made a move toward the men, but Lieutenant Krinn waved them back, and pulled Mr. Robinson away. "Take it easy, Robinson," he said calmly. "Let me handle this."

Melissa admired thte lieutenant's stern, no nonsense manner.

Mr. Robinson sat down gripping the arms of the chair, his face still filled with uncontrollable anger.

"Okay, Cannon," Lieutenant Krinn said, "You admit you picked up the ransom?"

Cannon nodded miserably.

"And your gangster friends have the boy. Where is he?"

"I'm trying to tell you," Cannon said. "I needed money—bad. When I rode with the posse I saw an opportunity—one desperate chance to save my life." He sent a pleading look to Mike Robinson. "I was mortgaged to the hilt—owed thousands on my credit cards, borrowed on my insurance, and I had to pay those gangsters by tomorrow."

"So you kidnapped Scott and held him for ransom," declared Lieutenant Krinn.

"I made the ransom call. From the motel," Cannon admitted in a quivering voice.

Then he dropped a bombshell.

"But I did not kidnap Scott!"

Everyone in the room stared at Roscoe Cannon, as he put his head in his hands and wept. After a moment, he took out a handkerchief and wiped his eyes. "Please believe me, Mike," he pleaded. "I wouldn't harm your boy for any amount of money."

With Scott's mother dead, Mr. Robinson seemed to be suffering enough for two. Anger swept his face again as he stood up and shouted at Cannon, "Then where is my son? Where is Scott?"

Cannon shook his head. "I don't know."

Lieutenant Krinn stared into Cannon's eyes. "You lied about the ransom. Why should we believe you now? *Where is Scott Robinson?*"

"I told you. I don't know!"

"Your friends are holding him until you bring the money. You don't want to rat on them. Isn't that it?" he prodded.

When Cannon didn't answer Lieutenant Krinn said, "It may take a while for you to remember. I'd better take you in. Maybe then you'll remember."

"It's no use. I've told you everything I know," Cannon said.

"He's guilty all right," the lieutenant said to Mr. Robinson. "But he won't talk because he's scared."

"Give me a lie detector test," Cannon said. "I'll prove I didn't kidnap the boy."

"You're going to tell us where you hid Scott—or else!"

The lieutenant was losing his cool. He turned to Detective Price. "Handcuff him."

The detective nodded and put on the handcuffs while Cannon, protesting his innocence, shouted, "I want to call my lawyer."

"You'll call from the station," said the lieutenant. "Let's go." He led Cannon out to a waiting squad car.

Melissa and Daniel were silent as they walked the snowy path to the hitching post. Butterball nickered and threw his head as they approached, and Socks echoed with a loud whinny.

"Something's not right about Cannon's arrest," Melissa said, reaching into her jeans pocket for a carrot. Breaking it in half, she offered a piece to each horse. "I wish I could put my finger on it."

"Well, Cannon admitted he made the ransom call," Daniel pointed out. "And we saw him pick up the money."

"That part is okay," Melissa said, tightening Butterball's cinch strap. "Yet I'm not too sure he knows where Scott is."

It began snowing again. Daniel swung up into his saddle. "Lieutenant Krinn thinks he's got his man. He even called off the search."

Melissa mounted and reined in beside him. "Daniel, do you think Cannon is his man?" she asked, tasting snow on her lips.

Daniel thought a minute. "Who else could it be?"

They started down the trail. "I don't know," Melissa said. "But just suppose that Cannon is telling the truth. The scenario would read that Cannon was desperate for money because of his gambling debts. When he learned Scott was missing, in order to save his life, he made the ransom call and collected the money. He buried the pouch and planned to dig it up tomorrow to pay off the gangsters who have his marker."

Daniel's eyebrows shot up. "And he had *nothing* to do with the kidnapping?"

"Nothing."

"I don't know if I buy that." Daniel's forehead puckered in a frown. "If Cannon is telling the truth, then where is Scott?"

She shrugged. "That's what I'd like to find out."

CHAPTER 8

Sunday—Noon

A new thought struck Melissa. She pulled the reins and stopped Butterball.

Daniel trotted over. "What's up?"

"I just remembered something," she said, as they walked their horses side by side.

"About what?"

"About Montana. The way he looked when he slipped into the kitchen yesterday. I thought at the time he had a rather mournful look on his face. But now I think it was more than that."

"What do you mean?"

"Well, it's hard to explain. He looked as if . . ." she searched for the right words. "He looked as if he knew something and he wasn't telling."

"He seems like a good guy."

"Oh, he is. But there's something strange and secretive about him. I can't quite put my finger on it. Mrs. Seliber even suspected him of stealing food last week. She was missing some fruit, and crackers and stuff."

"So the guy has light fingers. That doesn't make him a kidnapper—he seems to like Scott a lot," Daniel said.

"Yeah. Scott spends more time with Montana than he does with his own father," said Melissa.

"Maybe that's a clue."

Exactly what she was thinking.

They were heading out of the Robinson's front gate when a squirrel scampered up a tree trunk in front of them.

Melissa reined in, turned to Daniel and said, "Let's go back and check out Montana's home."

"I'm game. Where does he live?"

"In a cottage behind the Robinsons' house."

"Didn't the police search there?"

"I don't know. But it wouldn't hurt to check there again."

Melissa looked up at the sky. It was snowing harder now. It hadn't really stopped snowing the entire weekend. She pulled her hat over her ears again. It was always sliding up. "Let's get going. It's a good time to nose around. Montana usually does his barn chores about now."

They turned the horses and headed down the path to Montana's home.

"It used to be a guest house," Melissa said, as the snow-topped flat-roofed cottage came into view.

"What do you think we'll find here?" Daniel asked, as they tethered their horses.

Melissa dropped her voice. "Maybe a trap door to the basement where he's hidden Scott—or a closet with a secret panel—on TV . . ."

Daniel threw his head back and laughed. "Are you a TV addict—*or what*?"

She gave him a disgusted look and pushed the bell.

They could hear the first few bars of the old cowboy song, "Home On the Range," echoing through the cottage. Melissa remembered how pleased Montana had been when Mr. Robinson had given him the musical doorbell last Christmas.

"Why ring the bell?" Daniel asked.

"To make sure he wasn't home."

"What if he was?"

"I'd just say I came to ask about Nosey. She was supposed to be sick," Melissa reminded him.

"That's cool," Daniel said. "You sure can think fast on your feet."

She smiled, and rang the doorbell again.

As "Home On The Range" pealed once more, Daniel asked, "Have you ever been inside?"

"No."

"Well, he's obviously not home. Now what, J. B. Fletcher?"

Melissa ignored the fact that he called her by the name of the writer-detective in the TV series, "Murder, She Wrote." She just stood there and rattled the doorknob.

"It's locked," Daniel said.

"There's a door in back leading to the basement," Melissa said, "C'mon."

As they started to go around the cottage, there was a sudden shout from behind. "Hey, you two!"

Melissa's spine stiffened.

"Montana!" She threw a scared glance at Daniel.

"What do ya think yer doing?" From Montana's firmly pressed lips and the scowl on his lined face she could tell that he wasn't happy to see them.

"We were wondering about Nosey," Melissa said. "So we came to ask you how she is."

The rigidity seemed to go out of his body. "Aw, the little critter's okay. She never was sick."

He was sticking to his story.

"Oh, Montana. I'm so upset." She was shivering now. It was part cold and part fright.

"A kidnapping ain't no Sunday school picnic," he said, taking a key from his pocket. Then his eyes lit up. "I'm sure glad they caught the critter that did it."

Daniel said, "Mr. Cannon claims he didn't kidnap Scott."

"Did you expect the coyote to admit it?" Montana said. "But that lieutenant will get the truth out of him."

He unlocked the door of his cottage.

They couldn't stand there much longer. It was snowing hard, and Daniel had begun to cough.

"You look cold," Montana said. "Want to come in and warm up?"

Surprised by the invitation, Melissa gave Montana a startled glance.

Although Daniel was still coughing, he nodded, and they followed Montana inside.

A fire burned in the living room fireplace, and a large moosehead hung over the mantel. Melissa noticed the handknit green afghan thrown across the arm of the lumpy old sofa, and the worn sheepskin slippers on the hooked rug beneath it.

"Hey, Montana, this is real nice," Daniel said. He had finally stopped coughing and was looking around.

Melissa walked over to the fire, stuffed her gloves in the pockets of her jacket, and put her hands out to warm them. It felt good. Glancing up on the mantel she saw a faded photo of a thin young woman with high cheekbones and braids. She had her arm around a dark-complected boy about Scott's age. They were laughing—real laughs, not the kind of smile that freezes on your face when someone says "cheese."

But it was a photo next to it that made her start. A picture of Scott riding Nosey!

Montana caught her staring. When he came over she smelled the familiar "horsey" odor she always associated with him.

"I'd like to bust that Cannon in the nose." Montana shook his fist. "He better tell the cops where he stashed Scotty."

Melissa had never seen Montana so agitated. She felt terribly guilty for suspecting him of the kidnapping, especially when he said, "The boy's like my own flesh and blood."

She didn't tell him that Daniel and she weren't convinced that Cannon was the kidnapper.

Montana sat in the rocker, she and Daniel took the couch. The old man rocked back and forth and gazed off into the distance. Then he said, "I picked Scotty's first pony— taught 'im to ride. The way I taught my own son."

He got up, opened the fireplace screen, took a large log from the carrier and put it on the fire. After fanning the flame with a bellows, he sank into the rocking chair again.

It seemed to Melissa that Montana had the same mournful look on his face as he'd had in the Robinsons' kitchen the day before. "Kidnappers should be strung up on the nearest tree," he said. And he kept rocking.

After another long silence Montana said, "I never told no one about what happened to my woman and my son." He pointed to the faded photo on the mantel. "But Scotty's kidnapping brought it all back something fierce."

Melissa sensed that Montana was about to tell them the story of what had happened to his family.

He began, "We called our boy Swifty—for Swift Runner. My wife was Injun."

Montana leaned back, and closed his eyes. "It was a good life out West." He smiled, and his face was crisscrossed with creases. "We had us a log house out near Billings. There were horses, and cows—oh yeah—chickens too. While I cowpoked on a nearby ranch, Swifty and my wife took care of our place. We was a happy family. Until— one night . . ."

From her seat on the lumpy sofa, Melissa watched Montana study his calloused palms. Then he clasped and unclasped his hands. It was as if a terrible, long-ago memory made it too painful for him to go on.

He got up and poked the fire. Melissa and Daniel waited for him to continue. Finally, he sat down again, cleared his throat and said, "One night, I came home after work and my woman was screaming out of her mind."

"What happened?" asked Daniel.

"Two mean hombres with six shooters ransacked the place looking for money, and they took our boy." He held his head in his hands. "We never saw Swifty again."

"And your wife?" Melissa said softly.

"Died. Of grief," he said.

In the silence that followed, Melissa didn't know what to do or say. Minutes passed, and Montana just sat there rocking with his eyes closed and his head between his hands.

She caught Daniel's eye. He nodded and stood up. Coming here was a dead end, Melissa thought. They'd brought back a lot of painful memories for Montana. After what had happened to his son, he never would have kidnapped Scott.

"Thanks for letting us come in and warm up, Montana," said Daniel, zipping his jacket.

"We appreciate it," Melissa said politely.

Montana raised his head and opened his eyes. He didn't say a word—just stared into space, seeming to forget that Melissa and Daniel were there. When he didn't rise from his chair, they let themselves out.

It was still snowing.

From the accumulation on her saddle seat Melissa estimated that it had snowed half an inch since they'd gone inside.

Butterball put his head down and playfully pushed against her. "Watch it there, Butterball," she said, laughing. "You don't have to knock me down just because you're glad to see me."

"Now what, Sherlock Holmes?" Daniel asked, as he swept the snow off Socks's saddle with his gloved hand.

"I don't know," Melissa said, brushing Butterball's saddle too. "But I don't want to give up the search for Scott."

Her stomach began to gurgle. She hadn't eaten all day.

As if he could read her mind, Daniel said, "How about something to eat first? I'm starved."

"All right," she said, leading Butterball to a log for mounting. "We can get a burger and coffee at the motel coffee shop near where grid one ended, and continue the search from there. Okay?"

"Sure."

As Melissa mounted she said, "Where did grid two end?"

"At the Boy Scout Camp," Daniel said, settling in his seat. "The cops searched the camp yesterday afternoon. It was closed tight."

Melissa tossed her head. "I know. But with the big house and those log cabins—there's a zillion places to hide a prisoner."

"They may have overlooked something," he agreed.

"What do you say we follow grid two along the river and up to the camp?"

He grinned. "We're partners aren't we?"

When Daniel didn't talk in the coffee shop, Melissa knew he had something on his mind.

After they'd been served she said, "A penny for your thoughts, Daniel."

He took a bite of cheeseburger and said, "Are you satisfied that Montana's not involved with the kidnapping?"

Her eyebrows shot up in surprise. "Of course. Aren't you?"

"Not quite."

She sipped the hot coffee and felt it go all the way down and warm her toes. "What does that mean?"

"Well, I know you like the old guy—I do too, yet . . ."

She waited for him to continue.

"Yet, I get the feeling that he's missing a bit in his bridle."

Melissa squirmed in her seat. She recalled Montana's mournful look and her earlier feeling that he was hiding something. But when he'd told them the story of his son's kidnapping, she'd figured that Scott's disappearance had brought back memories that Montana had found too painful to talk about until now. And that was the reason it had seemed as if he knew a secret.

"Listen to this script." Daniel put his cup down and looked into her eyes. "What if in some scrambled way Montana thinks Scott is his son, Swifty? You know the way he calls him Scotty?"

"He has this peculiar way of talking," Melissa pointed out, "stampede, buckeroo, hombres . . . I don't think that means anything."

"Listen. He lives alone. Doesn't have any friends. So he lives in the past a lot."

"I guess that's true," Melissa admitted.

"We don't even know his real name."

Melissa chewed her sandwich thoughtfully.

"Let's suppose," Daniel said, "that with his wife and son gone, he latches on to Scott. The kid's father neglects him, and with Montana's memory a little foggy at times, he begins to think Scott is Swifty."

"So?"

"So he squirrels Scott away somewhere to keep him safe—from the kidnappers."

Melissa shook her head. "I can't buy that. I think Montana's innocent."

"Well, what about the food that Mrs. Seliber said was missing?"

"What about it?"

"Montana took it to feed Scott!" Daniel said triumphantly. "I say it all fits."

"But the food disappeared *before* Scott left," Melissa said. "Montana may be a little forgetful—but most of the time his mind is pretty sharp."

Daniel dropped the subject.

Later, though, when they were paying the check, he said, "Remember when we left Montana's? He didn't even seem to notice. Couldn't he slip in and out of awareness?"

Maybe Daniel had hit on the truth. Yet Melissa didn't want to think so. There is something really sticky here though, she thought, some molasses added to the oats so to speak.

CHAPTER 9

Sunday 2:00 P.M.

Although it had stopped snowing, the wind had strengthened sharply during the time Melissa and Daniel were in the coffee shop. When they came out, it seemed much colder than before. They walked their horses along the section of the forest preserve trail Lieutenant Krinn had designated as grid two. At the bend in the river, Melissa's cheeks smarted from the wind. She promised herself that she would rub lotion on the chapped skin when she got home.

They searched the coves along the river, peered into hollow trees, and climbed up and down the steep embankment to investigate each and every possible place that a small boy could be hidden.

They found nothing.

Finally, the plowed bridle path ended, and they came to the Boy Scout Camp, which consisted of three log cabins and a two-story wooden house farther up the road.

Melissa reined in and stopped Butterball. "He couldn't be here, Daniel. The cabins are all boarded up."

Daniel groaned. "All three?"

"Nailed tight. See for yourself."

After he'd checked out the log cabins Daniel shook his head, "Man, nobody could possibly have taken down all those boards, gone inside, and nailed them shut again."

Disappointment overwhelmed Melissa. She had been confident that they'd find some clue as to Scott's disappearance. Now here they were near the end of grid two, and nothing was working out as she'd expected.

"I suppose the house is boarded up too," she said.

"There's only one way to find out," Daniel said.

Slowly the horses plowed their way toward the big house, breathing heavily as they broke trail through deep snow. By the time they reached the two-story frame house their woolly winter coats were stained with sweat.

Melissa and Daniel stopped their horses when they saw it. They stared at the dreary looking house with the paint-peeled shutters standing gray and forbidding against a marshmallow-white world. The wind howling around the house made Melissa shudder, and a chill ran the entire length of her body.

"Wow!" said Daniel. "This place looks like the last stop on the Siberian Pony Express."

Enclosed in thick, snowy foam sculpted by the hooting wind, the big gray house warned them to stay out.

"Well, at least it's not boarded up the way the cabins are," Melissa said. "We're going in. C'mon." She sounded more determined than she felt.

Daniel turned to her. "Are you sure you want to go inside?"

She nodded. Nothing was going to keep her from finding Scott. She turned Butterball into the snow-swollen driveway.

Daniel followed. "Good thing our horses have winter pads on their hooves," he said.

"Yeah, we'd never get through this if the snow was balling up under their regular shoes." Melissa slid off into snow up to her boot tops, threw the reins over Butterball's head and began walking him toward a nearby oak.

After a few hesitant steps, Butterball balked and put his ears back.

"C'mon horse," urged Melissa, pulling on the reins, "Move!"

"Wait. Look at his ears," Daniel said, jumping down. "He hears something."

"Maybe it's a deer."

"No. Listen."

"Sounds like a baby crying," Melissa said.

The wailing stopped and a sudden gust of wind whistled through the trees.

They jumped.

"It's probably the wind we heard," Daniel said.

"No. It's a human sound."

Daniel cupped his ear. "Well, I don't hear it now."

Then it started again, a single tone—high-pitched and eerie.

"I'll bet a bale of hay Scott's in there," Melissa said excitedly.

Although her fingers were cold and trembling, she haltered Butterball quickly and tied him to a tree. The little palomino wasn't himself. Throwing his head, and snorting, he pawed the snow nervously, and kept at it until the tree roots were exposed.

A bright red object tangled in the roots caught Melissa's eye. She bent down and picked it up. "Daniel!" she cried. "Come here! Butterball found something!"

"What?"

She held up a red mitten. "It's Scott's mitten! It matches his red scarf. The one I found in the barn."

"Scott is a smart cookie," Daniel said, fingering the icy mitten. "Must of dropped it on purpose. To alert the police."

"But the snow covered it up," she said, her breath coming rapidly. "A hostage did it in a story we saw about a month ago. But instead of a mitten, the woman planted an initialed hanky."

They locked glances.

"Do you think someone is guarding him?" she asked.

"Let's find out," said Daniel.

Daniel was a great partner. He was game to try anything.

Crouching low so they wouldn't be seen, they carefully circled the big house. But they found the first floor windows shuttered tightly and all the doors locked.

"No sign of forced entry," Melissa whispered.

"So how did they get in?"

She shrugged. "Maybe they had a key."

"Possible," said Daniel.

"Could be it was stolen from the Boy Scout office."

Daniel nodded. "No time to check it out now."

They heard the wailing again, thin and high.

Melissa and Daniel traced it to the back of the house. Then it stopped. In the quiet several black crows cawed noisily to one another high above them.

"We'll have to wait," Melissa said, "until we hear the sound again."

"I think it came from back here," said Daniel.

Melissa closed her eyes. They were very close to finding Scott—she could feel it in her bones. She hoped with all her heart that nothing would go wrong now. But what if they were too late, and he was dead? She hadn't let herself consider the possibility—until now. The waiting was unbearable. She almost willed the wail to begin again.

When it came, it was tiny and thin and it hung weakly in the air for a very short moment—and then it evaporated. Yet it was long enough for Melissa.

Her eyes flew open. "The basement!" she whispered, and Daniel nodded, his eyes full of excitement.

They raced down the steep flight of stone stairs. Melissa reached the door first. She yanked at the doorknob, but the door didn't budge.

"Look out, Melissa," Daniel said.

He took a running leap and kicked the door with all his might. Melissa admired Daniel's daring—doing exactly what the cops did in "Police Story." On TV the door always burst wide open, but not here. This door was very heavy and it was locked tighter than a bronco's stall. They couldn't open it no matter what they tried.

On the way up the stairs again Melissa spied the coal chute. She turned to Daniel. "What do you know about coal chutes?"

"Nothing much. Except they must have used coal to heat this house. Probably shoveled it down the chute to the furnace room." He pointed over his shoulder with his thumb.

"Think we could we get into the furnace room through the chute?"

Daniel shrugged. "I don't know."

They had reached the landing, and he looked at Melissa. "We're not exactly midgets," he said. "It might be a tight squeeze."

"C'mon Daniel, let's see if it's open." When Melissa saw the doubtful look on his face she said. "There's no other way."

"Well—okay," he said.

They went over to the coal chute. Melissa tugged open the door and gave Daniel a look of triumph. "It's open," she said. "I'll go first."

"If you make it, I'll follow you."

But when Melissa looked down into the basement, she hesitated. The chute was a narrow wooden slide and its end was shrouded in darkness. It wouldn't be easy to climb in. She was tempted to gallop Butterball straight to the police, tell them about the wailing they'd heard and forget about playing detective.

"Hey . . ." Daniel poked her shoulder. "What's happening? You chickening out?"

Melissa shook her head. "Of course not." She couldn't tell Daniel what she'd been thinking. They *had* to find Scott. It was the only way to prove she could do something right.

Taking a deep beath, she scrunched herself down as small as possible, and tried to force her body into the coal chute opening, but she couldn't make it with her bulky jacket. She took it off and threw it on the ground. Then she tried once again to crawl inside the small opening.

She was freezing, but she made it!

Sitting at the top, it reminded her of the water slide at Holiday Park, only she didn't see clear, blue, water ahead—just blackness. Her heart began pounding. Well, here goes, she thought.

Melissa lunged forward, slid down the chute, and landed with a bump on the cement floor. The furnace room was cold and dark—awfully dark. She couldn't see. And the room smelled as dusty as a horse arena after a barrel race. She wanted to call out Scott's name, but she didn't.

There was barely time to roll out of the way when Daniel's lanky body, without his jacket, came tumbling down beside her.

"Wow! It's dark!" he whispered.

Melissa got to her feet and whispered back, "A fine pair of sleuths. We didn't even bring a flashlight."

"It's daylight," Daniel said, jumping up. "How did we know we were going to land in a pitch dark furnace room?"

"Shhhh," said Melissa, grabbing Daniel's arm, "do you hear it?"

The wailing had started again.

"It's in this room," he said softly.

'I think it's coming from over there."

"Where?" he asked.

"There." She pointed to the far corner.

Uncertainly, they started forward. In the pitch darkness, Melissa put her hands out in front of her. They mustn't make any noise. If they did, it would warn Scott's captors that they were coming.

The wailing stopped and they stood still. Waiting. Waiting. Why didn't it begin again? Melissa's mind raced crazily. What if they'd come too late? They had to find Scott. Melissa struggled to control her harsh breathing.

Then they heard it again! Thin and weak, but the same pitiful little wail.

Anxious to reach the place where the wail was coming from, Melissa tripped and fell forward touching something wet and slimy. She gasped. In the darkness, the aroma of rotten apples hit her.

Helping her up, Danile stumbled over an unlit kerosene lamp. "The kidnapper must have left this food and stuff," he said.

They were getting very close to the wailing now. Thank goodness her eyes were becoming accustomed to the darkness. Then she heard the wail stretch into a word, "Ohhhhh."

Quickly she ran toward the sound, not caring if she made

noise. Not caring about anything except rescuing Scott Robinson from his kidnappers.

She found him lying on the floor on a blanket. He was very still.

"Scott!" Melissa said hoarsely.

"Is he okay?" Daniel asked.

"I don't know." Melissa was on her knees beside the prone figure. "Scott! Can you hear me? Scott! It's Melissa."

Scott was still dressed in the red nylon jacket he disappeared in. He opened his eyes fleetingly, and they could barely hear him whisper, "Melissa." Then he blacked out.

"He's unconscious," said Melissa, holding the boy close. "But breathing."

"Probably drugged," Daniel said.

They held a whispered consultation.

"It's quiet upstairs. I don't hear anyone walking around." Daniel said.

"The kidnappers must have gone out for a while." Melissa said. "The snow probably covered their tracks. We've got to get Scott out of here before they come back."

"Yeah, I know," Daniel said, "But how?"

Melissa bit her lip. "Think you can carry him up those stairs?"

"Try the door first," Daniel suggested. "See if it's open."

Melissa laid Scott's inert body down carefully on the blanket. Taking one last look at him she felt her way up the stairs to the first floor door.

She tugged at the doorknob frantically. "Locked and bolted. From the outside," she said, coming down.

"How do we get him out of here then?"

She shook her head. "I'm fresh out of ideas."

CHAPTER 10

Sunday 3:00 P.M.

"This is unreal. Unreal," Daniel said, shaking his head. "They could come back any minute."

"We'd better think of something. Quick!" Melissa said. She pursed her lips and stared at the coal chute slide. "Guess the only way out is the way we got in."

"Yeah," Daniel said.

"Listen, I could walk up," she said, "You know—the way a kid does on a playground slide. When I'm out, I'll throw you my lead rope. Tie it on Scott and we'll hoist him up the chute. What do you think?"

Daniel didn't have to think. "Get going," he said.

Melissa grabbed the sides and started up the wooden chute. She took a few hesitant steps, and felt herself slipping. With wet boots, it was impossible to hang on. Letting go, she slid down on her belly.

"Guess it's tougher than it looks," Daniel said, helping her to her feet.

"You'd better believe it!" Melissa said. "Wet boots don't help." She dried the bottom of her boots on her pants legs.

"Going to try again?"

"Yep." Taking a deep breath Melissa started up the chute. Once more she gripped the sides and moved cautiously. Keep going, she told herself. Don't look back—you'll get dizzy. Step by step she went until she almost reached the top. All at once there was a sudden gust of wind howling around the building that shook the old house to its foundation. Melissa jumped back and lost her balance. Plopping on her seat, she slid all the way down to the basement floor.

"Dammit!" she muttered. "I was almost there."

"You hurt?" Daniel asked, helping her up again.

"Only my dignity," she said, dusting her bottom.

"Maybe I should go up first," Daniel offered.

"I've thought of that," said Melissa, "but you're stronger. If I'm having a problem getting up there alone, I'd never be able to make it carrying Scott." She squared her shoulders. "Here I go again."

For the third time, Melissa grabbed the sides and started up the chute. She'd better make it now. The kidnappers could come back at any moment.

One foot after the other. That's the way. Slowly but surely she was making progress. She looked up. Just a few more steps and you're there, she told herself. With her heart racing, Melissa finally reached the coal chute door.

Melissa hoped that she would be strong enough to open it. It was a small opening, but a very heavy door. She gave a tremendous push against it with her right hand, holding on to the side of the chute with her left. It didn't move!

Once more she pushed against it with all her strength. She was determined. Come on door—open, she prayed, we've got to get Scott out of here. Please. Please! Again she pushed with all her might, and little by little the door slowly opened. She heaved a sigh of relief, and climbed out.

"Whew! I made it!" she called down the chute, breathless from exertion.

"Good!" Daniel said, hoarsely. His voice sounded as if he was in a tunnel. "I've got Scott here. Now throw me the rope."

Brrr, it was cold. Melissa picked up her jacket from the snowy ground, put it on without bothering to zip it, and ran over to where Butterball was tethered. Quickly she untied her lead rope and hurried back to the coal chute.

"Is Scott okay?" she called to Daniel.

"I don't know. He's still out. Lower the rope."

Melissa leaned over and threw it to Daniel. Because of her bulky ski gloves, she almost lost her end, but she managed to hang on.

"Got it!" Daniel said.

After a few tense minutes of waiting Melissa looked down and said, "What's taking so long?"

"Hold your horses," Daniel said. "I'm tying Scott with the rope."

"Hurry!" she called.

Finally she heard Daniel say, "Okay. That should do it. I'll have to push him with one hand and grip the side with the other. You pull, I'll push, and we'll sort of slide him up together."

"Okay, Say when." Melissa knew pushing Scott up the chute would be a tremendous effort for Daniel. It had been hard enough for her to get up by herself.

"Now!" cried Daniel.

She leaned over and tugged the rope. Although he was a small boy, Scott, unconscious, was a dead weight. Melissa lost her hold on the rope, and felt it going. "Catch him!" she cried, as it slipped through her hands.

"Got him," Daniel said.

"Sorry," Melissa called down. "I'll take off my gloves—they're slippery."

"Your hands'll freeze."

"No time for debate. Send him up."

As Melissa pulled the rope with bare hands, Scott's limp body began to move ever so slowly up the chute.

"That's it. Keep going," Daniel said.

By the time Scott's head was near the top, Melissa's hands were raw and nearly frozen. Yet she kept pulling with all her strength.

One last push from Daniel and Melissa had her arms around Scott. As Daniel climbed out, she laid Scott's inert body in the snow. The boy's eyes fluttered when he reached the cold air. Then they closed. There was a blue lump as big as a quarter on his forehead.

"Oh, Scott. You poor kid," said Melissa, tenderly touching the lump. She felt tears forming. "Look Daniel, they hit him pretty hard."

"Those lousy gangsters!" said Daniel, putting on his jacket.

"Well, we can't let him lie here unconscious in the snow. He needs a doctor. Untie him and we'll get him out of here. In a hurry," said Melissa.

While Daniel was untying Scott, Melissa thought about how to get the boy home.

"We can tie him on a horse the way they did an outlaw in an old John Wayne western," she said.

"I don't think it'll work," said Daniel. "Most horses are too skittish—like Socks."

"Not Butterball. Last week Kory and I rode him double. No problem."

"Well, okay. We can't keep Scott lying here in the snow.

So let's try it. Mount up, quick!" Daniel told her. "I'll use the same rope and tie him onto your saddle."

With her gloves on again the feeling came back to her fingers. They tingled as Melissa brought Butterball over.

"I'll sling Scott across Butterball's withers. You hang on to him."

Melissa climbed into the saddle and said, "Don't *sling* him. He's hurt."

"Just a figure of speech," Daniel said. He lifted Scott, gently placed his limp body face down across the saddle in front of Melissa, and tied him on. Then he mounted Socks.

Melissa looked over her shoulder to see if anyone was following as they started off.

Although they were walking slowly, Scott kept slipping. Melissa was afraid she couldn't hold on to him. "Daniel, this is no good. We'd better tie him in back."

"It'll probably be better that way." Daniel dismounted, and tied Scott in back of Melissa's saddle.

"That's fine," she said. "He's more secure there."

Butterball kept turning his head and looking back at them. The little palomino seemed curious as to what was going on. He'd never carried an unconscious person before.

Several times during the two mile trip, Scott roused and whimpered. Once he gave a high pitched wail as he had done when he was locked in the furnace room. Melissa turned and patted his back. "You're safe now, Scott. Don't worry. Melissa's here. I'll never let anything happen to you, ever again."

It wasn't easy for Butterball. Because of the snow and the extra weight, he was breathing hard. They had to stop several times and let him rest.

Melissa wished they could get away faster. "Why don't you race ahead and alert the police at the Robinsons'?" she told Daniel. "I can't push Butterball any faster."

"No," Daniel said. "I won't leave you and Scott alone in the forest preserve. The kidnappers could come back to the house, find him missing, and follow the horses' tracks in the snow."

So they went along together. To Melissa it seemed much longer than a two-mile trip.

She breathed a sigh of relief as the Robinsons' barn came into view. She was never so happy to see a place in her whole life.

"Mr. Robinson! Mr. Robinson!" she cried, as they entered the yard.

Daniel dismounted, threw Socks's reins over the hitching post, and raced up the back stairs. "We found Scott!" he shouted.

The kitchen door flew open and Scott's father and Detective Price, both jacketless, ran down the stairs. Mrs. Seliber, buttoning her red wool sweater, wasn't far behind. Then the barn door creaked open, and Montana came running.

"Is he all right?" yelled Mike Robinson, his glasses fogging up in the cold.

Melissa and Daniel exchanged glances.

"We think so. Except for a bump on his forehead." said Daniel.

"Thank the Lord," boomed Mrs. Seliber. Her voice could break a glass, Melissa thought.

"Where did you find him?" asked Detective Price.

"At the Boy Scout Camp," Melissa said, dismounting.

"That's strange," said the detective. "Our men covered the entire area—cars, copters, the whole bit. Everything was boarded up."

"Not the big house," Daniel said. "He was on the floor in the furnace room."

"We got in through the coal chute," Melissa said.

The detective shook his head. "Wow! And how did you get him out?"

Daniel smiled. "The same way."

"And was there anyone else around?"

Melissa shook her head. "They were probably coming back any minute."

"I'll call Lieutenant Krinn and tell him the good news. I know he'll want to ask you some questions."

Detective Price ran up the stairs two at a time.

Scott moaned.

"Welcome home, little maverick," Montana said softly, patting Scott's head.

Mr. Robinson untied his son and gently lifted him from the horse. "Thank you kids. You don't know what this means to me. Getting my boy back alive."

Melissa kissed her horse's nose and said, "Butterball's the one who deserves the credit. He found Scott's mitten. And he carried us both home." She searched her pocket for a piece of carrot and gave it to Butterball. When Socks whinnied, she laughed and found a piece for him too. "Here Socks," she said, "don't be jealous."

Scott wailed again—high and thin.

"I'd better get him in the house," said Mr. Robinson.

Cradling Scott in his arms, he said, "You're okay now, son. Dad is here." He winced as he touched the discolored lump on Scott's forehead. And with his face grim he said, "They can't hurt you anymore." Then he carried Scott up the stairs into the family room and gently laid him on the sofa.

The others followed.

Melissa heard Detective Price on the phone in the other room.

"They found him in the furnace room. Yep. No sign of the kidnappers. Send the squads there? Will do."

Detective Price came into the family room. "Before we can wrap up the case, Scott has to identify Roscoe Cannon. The lieutenant is bringing him here shortly."

Mr. Robinson wrinkled his brow. "I don't know if he can talk."

He shook Scott's shoulder. "Son," he said softly, bending over the still little figure on the sofa. "Son, can you hear me?"

Scott's eyelids moved rapidly, in a nervous, excited way. He was opening his eyes!

The look on his face was a mixture of fear, bewilderment, and relief. He stretched out his thin arms and clung to his father.

"Daddy! Oh, Daddy!" He pressed his face against his father's chest. Then he fell back, unconscious.

"Scott!" Mr. Robinson shook his son by the shoulders. There was no response.

"He's out cold. I'm taking him to the hospital. Somebody call an ambulance!" he cried.

CHAPTER 11

Sunday: 5:00 P.M.

Scott lay unconscious in the red and white ambulance. A paramedic held an oxygen mask over his face. Beside them, Scott's father watched anxiously. Then the driver of the ambulance closed the door and Melissa couldn't see them anymore. She and Daniel climbed into the back seat of Detective Price's police car for the ride to the hospital.

The ambulance siren blared and its lights flashed as they rolled through the nearly empty Sunday streets. After what seemed to Melissa like a million years, the ambulance pulled up at the hospital emergency entrance.

Melissa and the others stood on the sidewalk while the attendants took Scott, still unconscious, from the ambulance on a stretcher. They followed the stretcher inside, where Scott was placed on a cart, and watched him being rolled down a long, gray hall to the X-ray room. Detective Price stationed himself outside the door. It was just like "General Hospital," the TV soap, Melissa thought.

After Mr. Robinson had talked to the admittance clerk,

and filled out some papers, he went with Melissa and Daniel to the empty waiting room.

When they were seated, Mike Robinson laid his head back against the wall and closed his eyes.

Poor man, thought Melissa. Those kidnappers put him through a terrible couple of days. Thank goodness it was all over and Scott was home.

"Scott will be all right," she said.

"These doctors know what they're doing," said Daniel.

Mr. Robinson opened his eyes and turned to them, his forehead wrinkled with worry. "I hope you're right." He took off his glasses, and rubbed his eyes. Melissa noticed how red they were from lack of sleep.

"I want to hear all about Scott's rescue." he said, putting on his glasses again. "You said you found him at the Boy Scout Camp?"

Daniel nodded. "It was Melissa's idea to keep searching for Scott."

"I couldn't have done it without Daniel," Melissa said, smiling at her partner. "We started at the end of grid one— where the posse left off, and ended up at the Boy Scout Camp."

"Didn't the police search there?" asked Mr. Robinson.

"Guess so," said Daniel. "But the cabins were boarded up, and the big house was locked tight. Unless they heard Scott wailing they wouldn't have known anyone was in there."

"Actually it was Butterball who first heard Scott crying," said Melissa. "And it was Butterball who dug up his red mitten."

"That's right," Daniel said. "Then we traced the wailing to the basement."

As they spoke, Melissa kept remembering Scott's pale face. Would he be all right?

"But how did you get in if all the doors and windows were locked?" asked Mr. Robinson.

"It wasn't easy," Melissa said. "We got in through the coal chute."

"You two went into the basement through that little coal chute?" Mr. Robinson shook his head. "Then how did you get Scott out?"

"We tied him with a rope, and while Melissa pulled the rope, I pushed him up the coal chute slide."

"Amazing!" said Mr. Robinson.

"And then Butterball brought him home—to freedom," Daniel said.

When they'd finished their story, Mr. Robinson said hoarsely, "Thanks, kids. I won't forget this. You don't know what it means to me to have my son back." His voice faded away as if he didn't have enough energy to go on talking. Melissa understood. After two days of worrying and being afraid for Scott, she was tired too.

Mr. Robinson asked, "Was there any sign of the kidnappers?"

"None," said Daniel.

"They had gone. But we were afraid they would be back soon," Melissa said.

When she saw Mr. Robinson's mouth tighten she said softly, "They gave Scott a blanket. And there was food."

"And I saw a kerosene lamp," Daniel put in.

"But the lump on his forehead." Mr. Robinson shook his head. "That's probably what caused him to black out. I hope it's not serious. That lousy Cannon and his cronies! When I see the miserable, lying . . ." He wrung his hands as if he had Cannon's neck between them.

In the silence that followed, Melissa heard the soft footsteps of the nurses going about their duties. They were sometimes punctuated by the loudspeaker paging a doctor.

The door of the waiting room opened and a slender, Asian-looking woman in a white coat came in. "Mr. Robinson?"

Mr. Robinson jumped up.

She walked over to where he was sitting and held out her hand. "I'm Dr. Luu."

They shook hands.

"How's my son, doctor? How's Scott?" asked Mr. Robinson.

"He has a mild concussion, and a few bruises." She smiled. "He'll be all right though."

"Thank goodness!" Mr. Robinson let his breath out in a sigh of relief. "When may I see him?"

"In a few minutes. After I treat the bruises."

"Can I take him home then?"

She brushed a strand of dark hair away from her eyes. "No. I want to keep him here overnight." When she saw the worried look on Mr. Robinson's face she touched his arm. "It's just a precaution."

"You're the doctor," he said as he sat down.

Just as Dr. Luu left, the door opened again. Lieutenant Krinn brought in Roscoe Cannon. Cannon's eyes were sunken with fatigue, and there were handcuffs around his wrists.

With clenched fists, Mr. Robinson shot to his feet and made a menacing move toward Cannon. "You filthy, lying buzzard!" he shouted.

His anger would have burned asbestos.

Lieutenant Krinn grabbed Mr. Robinson's shoulder. "Take it easy, man. Fighting won't settle anything." The lieutenant motioned toward a chair. "Sit down. Let me get to the bottom of this."

Mr. Robinson hesitated, then with eyes glaring, sank into his chair.

"First of all, how's your boy?" the lieutenant asked.

"Thanks to his friends," Mr. Robinson said, pointing his finger at Cannon, "Scott's got a concussion."

"Will he be okay?" Lieutenant Krinn asked.

Mr. Robinson nodded. "I hope so."

"Good! When he identifies Cannon here we'll . . ."

Roscoe Cannon jumped up. "You've got to believe me Mike," he pleaded, "I admit I made the ransom call. I was desperate! You don't know how it feels to be losing everything. *Everything!*"

Mr. Robinson stood and looked Cannon in the eye. "My son *is* everything to me," he said tersely.

"I'm no kidnapper! I never touched the boy!"

"Shut up, Cannon!" said the lieutenant. "Maybe you didn't personally—but some of your friends did."

"Jail is too good for vermin like you," Mr. Robinson said, and he sat down again.

"Why won't you believe me?" Roscoe Cannon asked.

Mr. Robinson turned away, and Lieutenant Krinn began to question Melissa and Daniel.

After they'd told him the entire story he said, "Good work, kids. Now all we need is for Scott to identify Cannon, and we can file formal kidnapping charges." He turned to Cannon. "And we'll find your confederates, too."

Cannon opened his mouth as if he was going to protest again, but then closed it without saying anything. He looked as tired as Mr. Robinson. And scared.

They sat in silence for several minutes. What was taking the doctor so long? Could Scott have taken a turn for the worse? The sound of Lieutenant Krinn cracking his knuckles made Melissa want to reach out and stop him.

Finally a young nurse came in. She looked around the room. "Mr. Robinson?"

Mike Robinson jumped up. "Here," he said, as if he were answering role call in a horse show.

She gave a flicker of a smile. "Doctor says you may see you son now. But just for a few minutes. He needs to rest."

"We'll all go in," said the lieutenant.

The nurse frowned. "Doctor Luu said only Mr. Robinson."

"Can you come back tomorrow?" Mr. Robinson asked Lieutenant Krinn.

"We won't disturb Scott," the lieutenant reassured Mr. Robinson. "Just a few questions, and we'll be able to put Cannon behind bars."

The nurse insisted that she'd have to ask Dr. Luu whether it would be all right for anyone besides Mr. Robinson to see Scott.

"Well, you can find out about the others," Mr. Robinson told the nurse, "In the meantime, I'm going in."

When Mr. Robinson and the nurse left, the lieutenant, cracking his knuckles nervously, sat down beside Cannon.

Immediately, Cannon began to plead with Melissa. "You know me, Melissa—we live next door to each other—you're our baby-sitter—haven't I always treated you well?"

She nodded.

"So how can you say I'm a kidnapper?"

Melissa looked at Daniel, then at her hands in her lap, and said quietly, "We saw you pick up the ransom."

"Sure, I picked up the money. I already told you that. But I promise you, I didn't touch Scott," he said. "Nor do I know who did."

Melissa looked at Cannon's handcuffs. They had made red marks on the flesh around his wrists. She was beginning to feel sorry for him. But then she remembered how at first he had tried to bluff his way out of his predicament. He'd even said *she* was lying.

"Melissa!" Cannon pleaded.

She was grateful that she didn't have to answer. The nurse had returned and she was coming in the waiting room door. "Dr. Luu said you may all go in now. Scott was asking for Melissa. But please don't stay too long."

The lieutenant nodded and motioned to Melissa and Daniel. They followed the nurse into Scott's room.

Scott's face was whiter than the bleached sheets. His hair was matted down and on his right cheek, below the bandage on his forehead, two bruises were turning blue. Mr. Robinson was seated on the edge of the bed.

When Scott saw Melissa, his face was a mixture of fear and relief. "Missy!" he cried, holding out his thin arms.

She hugged him fiercely. "I'm so glad you're safe."

"I'm fine, Missy," said Scott. "Don't cry."

Then Scott himself began to tremble and tears gushed out. His shoulders heaved as he cried great gulping sobs.

Melissa's vision was blurring. She straightened up and looked at Daniel. He grasped her hand and held it tightly.

Lieutenant Krinn thrust Roscoe Cannon toward the foot of the bed. "I know you've been through a lot, Scott," he said, "but I've got to ask you some questions."

Scott looked up at the lieutenant, teary-eyed. For the first time he seemed to notice the others who were present.

Lieutenant Krinn said, "Scott, is your kidnapper in this room?"

An ambulance siren blared outside while they waited silently around the hospital bed for the boy to answer.

It was a setting for the TV movie of the week, only this time Melissa was one of the actors.

Slowly, Scott looked into the face of every person in the room.

Did his eye seem to linger a little longer when he came to Roscoe Cannon?

Scott's entire body began to shake. "Kidnapper?" he finally said in a weak voice.

"The injury may have affected his memory," observed the nurse.

Mr. Robinson put his hand on Scott's arm. "Son." His voice was soft, and he spoke slowly and distinctly as if Scott was a lip reader. "When you didn't come home on Saturday morning, the sheriff called out the posse. To search for you. Later, I got a phone call from your kidnapper. He asked for fity thousand dollars. Ransom."

Scott's eyes rolled in his head. He looked as if he were about to black out again.

"Don't be afraid, son," his father said. "They can't hurt you now."

Sweat ran down Scott's face and hysterical sobs engulfed him again. He couldn't catch his breath.

"Daddy," he cried. "Oh, Daddy!"

His father took him into his arms and stroked his head. "You're safe now, son." He gave Roscoe Cannon a threatening look. "Nobody will ever hurt you again. Tell us—who kept you prisoner?"

"It was Cannon. Wasn't it?" said the lieutenant.

Scott took a huge gulp of air. Then, in a tiny voice, he said, "No."

Melissa gasped. If Cannon was clean who did that leave? Montana?

"I told you so!" Cannon shouted triumphantly.

"Then, who?" prodded Lieutenant Krinn.

Scott's eyes darted around the room once more.

Melissa held her breath and clung to Daniel's hand as Scott finally said in a half whisper, "I wasn't kidnapped."

Daniel and Melissa stared at each other open-mouthed.

"What?" shouted the lieutenant. "Say that again." He cracked his knuckles loudly.

Scott's face was sweating, and his lips trembled. He tried to speak but the sound that came was just a whisper. "I wasn't kidnapped. I ran away."

Mike Robinson was speechless. He looked as if he didn't believe his ears.

Scott looked at his father pleadingly, "I only meant to stay out overnight."

Mr. Robinson touched his son's bandaged forehead. "But your bruises—and the furnace room."

Scott spoke slowly, with many pauses, mostly to his father.

"I knew about the open coal chute door at the Boy Scout Camp. So I brought a blanket, food, and water there during the week." He paused, his eyes brimming with tears again.

That's where the food went, Melissa thought. Montana hadn't taken anything after all.

Scott blew his nose. "I pretended Nosey was sick," he continued. "When Mrs. Seliber called," now he looked directly at Melissa, "I put the light on in the barn—so you'd think I was still there, and I ran—the way that kid did in the Alfred Hitchcock mystery special."

"What about the red scarf and mitten?" Daniel asked.

"I was in such a hurry to get away, I lost my scarf somewhere. Later, I dropped my mitten. It was snowing so hard, I didn't have time to look for it."

"But your forehead . . ." Mr. Robinson said. "Who gave you that big lump—and the bruises?"

Scott swallowed hard. "When I slid down the chute, I lost my balance and hit my head on the cement floor." He fingered the bandage on his forehead. "I was so dizzy. I could hardly crawl over to the corner where I'd put my blanket and food. After that I don't remember anything. Except my head hurt. Something awful. And still does." He fell back on the pillow.

"That's why he kept blacking out," Melissa said.

Roscoe Cannon rattled his handcuffs. "I'm innocent. Take these off!"

"Innocent of kidnapping, maybe," said the lieutenant. "But not extortion. I'm still going to book you. Let's go."

"Thanks for everything, lieutenant," Mr. Robinson said. "You and your men did a great job."

"You should thank these kids, too," said the lieutenant, pointing to Melissa and Daniel. "They found him."

The lieutenant left with Cannon.

"I certainly do thank you two," Mike Robinson said to Melissa and Daniel. "You didn't give up, even after the police searched the Boy Scout Camp thoroughly."

Melissa and Daniel smiled at each other.

"I'm sorry, Missy," said Scott. "I didn't mean to cause you any trouble." His voice was full of apology. "Can we still be friends?"

Melissa went over and hugged the frail boy. "It was a hairy couple of days for me, Scott. But I'm glad you're okay. Sure we're friends. I care a great deal about you. So does Daniel . . ." She pointed over her shoulder to where Daniel was standing. "And Montana was worried out of his skull about you—Mrs. Seliber too."

"I was only going to stay out overnight." Tears were forming again. He turned to his father. "So you would really miss me." He buried his face on his father's shoulder.

"Of course I missed you," Mr. Robinson said. "You're the most important person in my life."

Scott's eyes lit up.

"I don't blame you, son," said his father. "It was all my fault. I kept telling myself that running away was just a phase you were going through. I didn't realize I was really neglecting you."

Scott lay back on the pillow, his face still white and pinched.

"Listen son," said Mr. Robinson, "I'm going to cancel *all* my business meetings for the next month to be with you. When you're stronger, we're going skiing."

Scott smiled, and he was all teeth.

"Now promise me you'll never run away again," said Mr. Robinson.

"Promise," Scott whispered. His father pulled the covers up around him, and he promptly fell asleep.

Mr. Robinson kissed his cheek. Then he turned and smiled. It was the first time he'd smiled since Scott had disappeared.

CHAPTER 12

Sunday, 7:00 P.M.

"If it hadn't been for you two—continuing the search for Scott . . ." Mr. Robinson said, shaking his head, "I don't know what might have happened to him."

Melissa and Daniel were in Detective Price's squad car with Mr. Robinson, and they were heading home. "I'm really grateful, kids," he said.

Melissa sighed. She was glad it was over, and Scott was safe. "Do I still have my baby-sitting job?" she asked.

"You sure do. But I'm warning you, Melissa," he said, with a wry grin, "I plan to stay home a lot more."

She recalled how Scott's face had lit up when his father had said they were going skiing, and Melissa felt good about it.

When the squad car pulled up at the Robinsons' house, the yard was flooded with light. Montana and Mrs. Seliber rushed out on the porch without their coats.

"How's our boy?" boomed Mrs. Seliber, hugging crossed arms to her ample chest.

"He's going to be fine," said Mr. Robinson, getting out of the car with Melissa and Daniel.

"Praise the Lord." Mrs. Seliber belted out the words like a gospel singer.

"And that scallywag Cannon?" said Montana, with a grimace that turned his face into a map of wrinkles. "Sure hope he gets his comeuppance."

"I'll be there in a minute and tell you all about it," said Mr. Robinson. "Go inside now—you'll freeze without coats."

Detective Price rolled down his window and said, "I'll be leaving now. I'm due back at the station."

"So long," said Mr. Robinson. "Tell Sheriff Leonard I really appreciate all the help you and the other men gave me." He smiled and waved as the detective pulled out of the yard.

Then turning to Melissa and Daniel he said, "Want something to eat before you go?"

"No thanks, I have to be heading home," Melissa said.

"Me too," said Daniel.

"I understand. It's been quite a weekend and everyone is tired." Mr. Robinson smiled. "You two are super sleuths." He gave a little salute. "See you on the trail." Then he slowly climbed the stairs and stamped the snow off his boots. He seemed weary, but in good humor.

For Melissa, all the bad feelings of the past two days were gone, and the tension eased. The weight of guilt was off her shoulders and she felt suddenly lighthearted and happy. As they walked toward the Robinsons' barn to get their horses, she realized that she was hungry. So much had happened in so short a time, and she hadn't eaten or slept much.

"I'm starving," she told Daniel as she hoisted herself into the saddle, and pulled the reins taut.

"Me too," he said, leading Socks to the mounting block. "I only had one cheeseburger today. I must be sick."

"Well, you do have a wretched cold. Isn't the old saying starve a cold . . ."

He grinned. "I think it's the other way around. You're supposed to feed a cold . . ." He gave a few fake sneezes.

Melissa giggled, and wheeled her horse in the direction of her home. Butterball sidestepped and bucked gently.

"Take it easy, old boy," she said, firmly reining in her horse. "You're not going to race for the barn in the dark." Yet, she understood her horse's impatience to get home. She wanted to get there quickly, too. Butterball had been tied in many places during the last forty-eight hours—at the Robinsons', in the cave, down the hill at the stakeout, at the Boy Scout Camp. And the little palomino had heard Scott crying, found his mitten, and carried the boy to safety. He deserved a whole bag of carrots for himself.

She stroked Butterball's silky, golden neck. He soon quieted and slowed to a walk.

Just before they came into her yard, she turned to Daniel, riding beside her. "Want to come in for pizza?" she asked. "We've got some homemade in the freezer."

"Sounds good."

In the Mansfield's kitchen over pizza and Cokes, they told Melissa's father and mother the story of how they had found Scott.

"So he ran away after all," Mr. Mansfield said, reaching for the red pepper. "I was sure he was kidnapped. Yesterday, I even suspected Montana."

Melissa and Daniel locked glances.

"I wondered about Mrs. Seliber," confessed Melissa's mother. "Her call asking you to take out the roast was an airtight alibi. But she could have had an accomplice."

"Roscoe Cannon seemed guilty to me. I bet on him all the way," Daniel said, munching the pizza.

Melissa sipped her Coke. "Well, you were half right. But golly, I was suspicious of everyone till the very last moment . . ." she giggled. "Even Daniel."

The others laughed.

"This pizza is super," Daniel said.

"Want another piece?" asked Mrs. Mansfield.

"Please," said Daniel.

"Me too," Melissa said.

As she watched her mother cut the pizza she asked, "Mom, do you really think Mr. Robinson will spend more time with Scott like he said?"

Mrs. Manfield wrinkled her forehead and thought about Melissa's question. "I'm sure Mike loves Scott. And he knows he's hurt the boy. But—well, when you're in business, Missy"—she pointed with the metal pizza cutter—"especially in the banking business—there are lots of pressures. Mike's lucky that he found out how much Scott was hurting before it was too late." She offered Melissa a slice of pizza on a wide spatula.

Before Melissa took a bite she said, "Well, Scott certainly put us through a terrible couple of days. All of us thinking he was kidnapped—calling the sheriff—the posse going out—Mr. Robinson paying all that ransom . . ."

"I agree. But maybe something good will come out of it now. If they talk to each other about their feelings, things should be better between them. Certainly not perfect," said her mother, "but better."

"Sure hope so," Melissa said. "Scott's really a good kid."

"What do you suppose will happen to Roscoe Cannon, Mr. Mansfield?" Daniel asked.

"Well, they found the ransom money, but he caused Mike

a great deal of anguish. He'll probably end up serving time."

"I feel sorry for his wife and kids," said Melissa.

The phone rang, and Mr. Mansfield jumped up. "I'll get it," he said, going into the family room.

In a few minutes, he returned smiling. "It was Mike Robinson," he said, standing in the doorway.

"What did he have to say, Chuck? I can see you're bursting to tell us," Connie Mansfield said.

"Sheriff Leonard asked him to be co-leader of the posse with me."

"It figures—since Roscoe won't be around," said Mrs. Mansfield. "But that's not what has you grinning like a Halloween pumpkin, is it?"

He shook his head and gave a little laugh. "You know me so well. Mike also said that Daniel and Melissa did a terrific job. That our daughter has a good head on her shoulders." His eyes sought Melissa's. "And I agreed with him."

It felt great to get a compliment from her father. Melissa glanced sidewise at Daniel and he gave her a V for victory sign.

"But that's not all," continued Mr. Mansfield, his blue eyes warm and crinkly the way Melissa loved to see them. "Our first act as coleaders is to ask Melissa Mansfield to be a permanent member of the sheriff's posse!"

"I don't believe it!" Melissa cried. She rushed at him, and with tears streaming down her face, wrapped her arms around her father. "Oh, Dad, you're one in a million!"

He held her close. "Well, hon, I think you're pretty great yourself."

Then she hugged her mom. She even hugged Daniel.

"I've got to call Kory." She ran to the phone and punched her friend's number. "Guess what?" she said breathlessly.

As she told Kory of the events of the past twenty-four hours, Melissa felt like a jockey who'd just won the Kentucky Derby.

When she returned to the kitchen, her mother and dad were pulling on their boots to go to the barn for evening chores.

"There is still something we haven't settled, Melissa," her mother said. "I think you know what it is. I don't want to spoil your evening, so we'll discuss it tomorrow. Okay?"

Melissa's face felt flushed. She knew it was about her punishment for sneaking out of the house. Well, she deserved to be grounded, but she hoped it wouldn't be for too long.

When Mr. and Mrs. Mansfield left, Daniel helped Melissa clear the table. After they'd put the dishes in the dishwasher, Daniel reached for his jacket.

"It's been a long day," he said. "I've got to get going."

"Are your folks coming home tonight?"

"Yep. Should be in any minute."

She walked him to the door.

He turned and looked deeply into her eyes. "Before I go, I want to tell you something, Melissa." He took her hand and squeezed it. "This was the best weekend of my entire life. You're an awesome partner."

Then he leaned over and kissed her gently on the lips.

She had a warm, wonderful feeling all over. How could she ever have thought of Daniel as a stupid beanpole? "You're not so bad yourself, Daniel." She put her arms around him and kissed him back.

He was beaming as he went out the door.

When Melissa was in bed that night, as tired as she was, she couldn't fall asleep. Thoughts were churning in her brain like food in a mixer. Daniel had said it was the best weekend of nis life—well, it had been quite a weekend for her too. Although Scott's bogus kidnapping had devasted her, in the end it had brought her a measure of self-respect.

She had finally been asked to be a permanent member of the posse! She was as pleased as could be. And so were her parents and Kory.

But best of all, she had a new friend—Daniel. He made her feel good—pointing out her best qualities instead of always telling her she was irresponsible.

People don't change overnight. She knew that. It would take time to be the person she wanted to be. But she'd do it—work on her good points, reprogram herself so to speak, for a good self-image.

Melissa thought about Daniel's kiss, and the warm glow it left her with. She liked him a lot. Maybe they would become a couple someday. They certainly worked well together.

She sighed, took a deep satisfying breath and pulled the covers up around her chin. For once Melissa Mansfield was in the Winner's Circle. And it felt good.

ABOUT THE AUTHOR

FERN BROWN lives in Riverwoods, Illinois. This is her third Fawcett Juniper novel. She is a former teacher and an established writer of both fiction and non-fiction for juveniles and young adults.

MORE POPULAR THAN EVER

Isabelle Holland